T5-AOL-082

Sleep Song

The Spell

Books by Doris Dix Caruso

SLEEP SONG (The Spell)

SERENITY IN SANDY SHOES Lyric Poetry

Sleep Song

The Spell

A Novella

by

Doris Dix Caruso

First Published in 1998

Copyright © 1998 by Doris Dix Caruso

All Rights Reserved

Published by Seashore Journals
P.O. Box 100,
Frisco, NC 27936

ISBN 1-57502-826-3

Printed in the USA by

MP
MORRIS PUBLISHING

3212 East Highway 30 • Kearney, NE 68847 • 1-800-650-7888

to my first and my "forever" love...
and for all of his indulgence.

******

How sweet the moone-light sleepes upon this banke.
William Shakespeare
The Merchant of Venice (1623)

******

As when great shipwrecks mark the tempest's might,
And planks and helms are tossing on the tide
With spars and prows and masts and drifting oars,
And many a hull goes floating by far shores,
A visible sign to mortals who would brave
The guileful ocean's treacherous strength and spite,
Bidding beware, nor evermore confide
In this false whisper of the windless wave.
Lucretius 96-55 B.C.
De Rerum Natura

******

Il descend, reveille, l'autre cote du reve.
Awakened, he descends the far side of dreams.
Victor Hugo
Ce Que Dit la bouche d'ombre
(1855)

Contents

Part I	The Sleep Song of Diarmaid and Grainne	1
	Cheers - *Slainte - Salud*	3
	Refuge	6
	Supervivencia - **Survival**	11
	Summer Has Come	14
	New Companions	17
	The Larger Family	20
	Shadows	22
	A Jaundiced Eye	27
	Montoac	29
	Hallucination	31
	Erotica	33
Part II	The Book of the Lays of Fionn	35
	Matrimony	37
	Wild Steeds *Garran*	43
	Gift	47
	Miracle	48
	Pardon	50
	Dialogue	52
	Fete	54
	Slight Knowledge	58
	Anguished	61
	Persuasion	62
	True Love *Asthor*	65
Part III	*Magh Mell*	69
	Deliverance	71
	Island Thoughts	73
	New Sails	76
	Magh Mell	79
	Lost and Found	81
	Flight	84
	Young Fool	86
	The Choice	89
	Secrets Shared	92
	Hoax	95
	Final Deception	97

Prologue

Fully realizing that it is not necessary to include a preface with a work of fiction, I believe it might be interesting for my readers to know something of what inspired this volume and therefore I offer this commentary.

When I walk on the sandy shore of the Atlantic Ocean, dunes, birds, sky and wind as my only companions, it is not difficult to place myself back in time, in this same landscape, decades, even centuries ago; for basically here at the seaside, nothing has really changed. Here, we all can permit our imagination to take charge and to energize our intellect for an idyllic interlude, a respite ... to dream a bit if we will.

Some readers will recognize the setting in Sleep Song as the low profile, narrow set of islands that we now call the Outer Banks, (Hatteras Island to Ocracoke, specifically.)

It is my hope that those who read this work will become as engrossed and infatuated by this fictitious tale as I have ...

for remember ... it could have happened so!

Part I

The Sleep Song of Diarmaid and Grainne

One of the most famous love stories of Irish literature is that of Diarmaid and Grainne. No manuscript copy exists earlier than the fifteenth century although the incidents on which the story is based may have been known in the tenth century. This story tells of Finn's intention to marry (in his old age) the young and beautiful Grainne who descends from Irish royalty. When she realizes that he is older than her father, she flees with Diarmaid whom she has put under a spell. The tale describes their wanderings on a far shore.

Grainne's character is unusual in Irish literature for she is both frivolous and selfish.

There is close parallel between portions of this story and that of Tristan and Isolde.

Grainne (or here Estrella) sings a sleep song for Diarmaid in which she wills him to sleep, though she notes that all the animals of the wilds are awake and restless:

> Sleep a little, a little little,
>   for thou needst not fear the least
>   lad to whom I have given love,
>   son of O Duibhne, Diarmaid...

Cheers - Slainte - Salud

Waves tossed foam high making definition of the cask not altogether certain, then as everyone stood only half sure of its identity, the vat was as suddenly flung up from the frenzied sea as if some great beast had released its prey only to be heaved heavily upon the rock hard sand, offering a solitary treasure for the band of bewildered survivors huddled there.

Could there have been any separate action as outrageous? The impulse of these six persons was spontaneous, all rushing to the blackened keg, seaweed and red bracken still hanging from its staves, as they in one fellowship rolled and pried the round drum about with the jovial shrieks of small children. For here in the loss of all other worldly belongings, this homely, singular vessel promised at least diverse prize in which they equally might share.

The long knife of the seaman was unsheathed, for in truth, the barrel was weighty with liquid, and the frenzy to know what it contained made near lunatic this adult assembly.

And what a dissimilar collection they were, there on a windswept, barren beach, no other creature or habitat in sight, only endless gray sky, wild pounding ocean, miles of shoreline and six sorely tattered, sodden human beings.

One could easily observe: two were plain, brutish and heavy men of the sea, coarse, bearded and rough, another a dark, fine featured, towering gentleman, recognized by his noble bearing and magnificent costume, despite its ruined appearance; yet another, a mature, proud woman clad all in somber black silk garments.

The only other female stood resolutely straight and prim aside the elder woman. She was a dark, young, exquisite creature, slight, beautiful, yet extremely tense and secret. Garbed in regal habit complete with ponderous golden jewelry about her neck and wrists, her graceful form did not waver its haughty countenance despite her plight.

The sixth and final member of the small band remained somewhat apart from the others. He, without doubt, was as young as his tall, strong body, pleasing features, and stately air suggested, but more was apparent here. The believable, certain attitude of his frame set him aloof in more than distance. The entire scene before him took shape as though he fully recognized his portion of the spectacle and with it, the total result giving him undeniable command. Alert, rigid and close to his right side stood an amazing wolf-dog of impressive bearing.

The cask was quickly righted, the bung removed, and a grimy finger lowered into its liquid depths. It could have been any store carried on a frigate now lost to a submerged, watery grave: a cask of black olives, one of cooking oil, pickles, or the red beets made into sweet, preserved delicacy. At once the heavy bearded man held finger to lips as wild exuberance burst from that shabby exterior. He held his index finger high, piercing the humid air, while taking a few steps to simulate the sailor's jig. Then raising his weathered face skyward, shouted raucously — so loudly that even the sea maws might hear:

"Cheers, my comrades, hallelujah! By heaven, 'tis sweet ruby port, aye, to all of ye, cheers!"

Ten full hours elapsed since that dramatic discovery. The euphoria presently was diminished, yet for some impassioned moments following the disclosure of those inebriant contents in the wine barrel, a certain fractious energy released by members of the company prevailed and continued for several hours as the precious contents were drunk by the persons in larger or lesser measure.

The small, black lacquered, locked chest lying close to the billowed skirts of the dark, younger woman was quickly but furtively opened, producing a golden cup, held in the small hand and persuaded forward to accept her share of wine. With one swift and gratified expression, following her quaffing of the drink, she passed the vessel to the older woman who in turn took a share. Then the stately gentleman was offered his refreshment while beaming the first smile this fellowship had seen that day from his dark, impassioned face. Pushing forward the golden cup to be filled anew and then standing, raising it aloft, he uttered a single word in toast, "Salud!," he said, so confirming the two brusque seamens suspicions were in fact accurate; this noble looking gentleman and his pair of female companions were of Spanish lineage as surely as the two gritty seamen were Dutch and their tall, young companion, as Irish as Saint Columba. For the sailors recognized that word, Salud, as portion of the language heard from the swarthy Spanish seafarers encountered in their countless, prior ports of call.

Perchance it was due to the spirits, who can say, for this day slipped by with some fanciful, intangible hope for the future. In order, the seamen set off to scour the beach for several miles in separate directions of the sandy shore, yearning to expose added booty on which to survive. The wine, while a pleasing suspension of physical anxiety, granted nothing to the six beings for subsistence nor for any forestalling of the deep hunger beginning to gnaw in each of their empty stomachs.

Our Irish and youngest sailor took off into the bleak, low sand dunes standing some two hundred feet from the shore, he having cordially declined the ruby port. His search, dictated by a reasoning only he could imagine, seemed imperative to the mandate of survival. The Dutch seamen separated to scout the rugged beach.

This left the three Spaniards, now seated on the squat driftwood, huddled together, speaking intently as that first long afternoon headed into dusk.

And now we have the setting: six dissimilar, shipwrecked humans on some foreign shore, saved by providence from a sodden grave, some of whom were not easily conversant with the others, either to make fear or feelings known, and an ominous darkness stealing in rapidly as they found no place to lay their weary heads.

Refuge

The time of the storm that brought these persons together, as fate would have it, was notably near the vernal equinox. This fact was known to them all, but it was only the Irish Diarmaid who kept exacting count of the days on a strip of wood cut from the live oak found in the thicket standing not far distant from the beach where the company had landed.

He, extremely familiar with record keeping, felt the act significant in his struggle to survive and fixed the date: 14 May, anno Domini, year of our Lord, 1630, recollecting that today marked exactly seven weeks since these six individual souls had been brought together in that violent storm.

Finally, the fellowship had come to support for one another, this lean-to shelter was constructed to keep out rain and coolness of night, a pit and cook-fire formed just outside it to prepare what wild game and fish the men caught, and a garden of sorts begun in a damp patch of earth within a small clearing of woods comprising a few recognizable plants of the forest.

******

Communication had been slow in coming, yet they now had established a manner of understanding through sign and an assortment of common phrases. Translating the Spanish to the Dutch to the Irish was not that difficult to fathom when it became necessary for a common existence, after all.

During the long evenings, when everything possible was accomplished in making provision for the little band, the following truths were made known: the two coarse seamen, along with the younger and more genteel one, were the only survivors of the Dutch merchant ship, Royal Rotterdam, lost to that terrible storm off this coast where they now existed. The elders were Hans and Jochim by name, who had been at sea for the greater portion of their lives and were related as cousins, sharing the same grandparents with homes in Amsterdam. Hans left wife and children, while Jochim was unmarried.

Just why destiny had singled only them of the crew to survive the torrent, they had no answer, except that they remembered working diligently to loosen halyards in order to take down the last remnants of sail as the gale discharged its greatest fury, and they recollected being cast backward together into the wild sea.

A great piece of wood, possibly some rail, was just in reach ahead of Hans as he came to water's surface, and he managed to secure himself and his cousin to it while waves pushed them on toward shore. That no other man of their forty crew had been saved perplexed them greatly. Hope for those who might have been tossed upon some other shore, far up or down this same beach and preserved, remained deep in their breasts, so much so that they planned an expedition during this week, exploring for some distance, both north and south along the coastline in search of survivors.

Diarmaid, the young, tall Irish lad was passenger on The Royal Rotterdam. He had embarked from Amsterdam many weeks earlier in search of an adventure in this newly discovered hemisphere. He tried to explain that somehow the land mystically drew his spirit. He said that he had neither relatives in the Netherlands, nor in the Ireland of his birth, and more detail of his life he seemed reluctant to disclose.

Neglecting to tell you that he had escaped the dreadful fate of being drowned by the aid of his wolfhound swimming to shore with Diarmaid clinging to his powerful neck makes the account less than precise. For yes, this band was made complete to seven by a magnificent dog-wolf of amazing vitality who stood near his master's side in constant vigilance. The mighty animal answered to the name of Bran.

As for the Spaniards, their's was an arresting tale. It had taken many nights following the evening meal, as the six sat circled on the pine straw floor of the lean-to, finally to make their thoughts known to the others in the completion of their story.

The towering dark gentleman was named Count Pedro de Mendenez, sent as direct emissary from Philip IV of Spain to protectively accompany the two women in his charge. The younger, Estrella de Valazquez, a noblewoman, was promised in marriage to the Governor-general of Cuba, Hernando de Altoras, at the port of Baracoa, its major settlement and Cuba's oldest province. Estrella had never met her betrothed, yet was committed in marriage to him by King Philip, himself.

Our sailors discovered, natural as it might seem, the captain of the Spanish ship, The Annunciation, was distressed to distraction by the sudden tempest driving its mountain of waves over his decks, and chose therefore to place his precious, royal consignment of three persons into a lifeboat just as the storm raged at its height. No sooner were they lowered into the dreaded sea and forced some distance from its bow than the entire vessel was thrown to its side as the horrified trio saw it sink before their eyes.

In what seemed moments, a huge wave carried them on its crest and landed their small boat upon this beach, crashing in its hull, only salvaged were the rich dowry and royal finery accompanying Estrella and the black coffer which had produced the golden cup. What other treasures remained in that guarded box was mere mystery to the survivors.

The older woman was a gentlewoman, chaperon and protector of the younger. Her name was Maria de Sanchez. She was servant in the household of the Valezquez family for many years. Although stiff and cool, she nevertheless seemed to have deep affection for the self-centered, yet ravishing young woman.

Now as Diarmaid reflected on these past weeks, he remembered how after the port was completely consumed and the canteens of drinking water were as emptied, they had all thirsted enormously, despite everyone sipping only drops at a time. So when a torrent of rain fell on their fourth night, they all rejoiced in this, the purest of God's gifts, blessed rainfall.

It was Diarmaid who observed that containers of a sort could be utilized by placing clam shells open to catch rain water, so he set about emptying hundreds of these into canteens as early as daylight in that first week, finding, if it had rained, this filled the flasks with pure water for at least three days. The surplus was placed in the barrel for emergency rations. He knew that this was an inefficient manner of gathering and he must soon find remedy, as the acquisition of fresh water was crucial for his little band to survive.

Yes, I said "his little band," for despite Diarmaid being but nineteen and by far the youngest of the six, he instinctively took on the role of leader early in the predicament. It was assuredly not a spoken thing, yet one altogether obvious to the understanding of all six of these unique survivors.

******

"¿cua'l es la fecha?" Estrella stood gazing over his shoulder as Diarmaid sat etching his wood bark with a stylus he had fashioned from a piece of sharp metal found on the beach. Curiously though, he understood her question.

"It is the sixteenth of May." he responded not looking up. Undeniably, the understanding of speech never studied was not that difficult to accomplish if one considers the attitude of the speaker and feels attune to her humor. Most probably it is much like the manner in which we first learn speech as children, yet at that tender age do not anguish over long on the period of interval required to make our words known.

Diarmaid mused that if remaining here long enough he might have full knowledge of the Spanish language, should his companions be inclined to speak with him, however thus far, Estrella was distant and aloof from all of them, so even with her own chaperon, Maria.

And really why not, what hope did any of them have for a shift in their plight, or was it plight if thy accepted it? Count de Mendenez certainly was not abandoning the crisis under which he found himself. Each night at dusk, he persisted in lighting a signal fire on the beach and not without considerable difficulty. Accomplished from the embers they kept aglow through every day, he managed this as some beacon; for whom and for what purpose Diarmaid could not imagine, except as some honorable fulfillment of the mission given to him by his king in quest of that task he swore to.

The appearance of any ship was indeed unlikely and even the viewing of one would not mean they might be seen by it. Undoubtedly, their disappearance would be thought of as only one of the many losses in the conquest of new lands and the habitation of the same.

By now in this beginning of the eighth week on land, Diarmaid became convinced it was best to dismiss any possibility that six persons would ever be transported elsewhere, and they should actively begin to seek a new life for each member on this bizarre, exotic sandy shore.

Supervivencia - Survival

Drinking water was ultimately not that difficult to find when the four men put their backs to it. They had only to construct several large wooden containers in which to catch a celestial bounty, as it was common for heavy rain to fall here about every four nights. The difficult portion of their task was in not having the right tools to complete the work, for the sailors possessed only long knives; yet finally as the four of them worked diligently, the results wrought by hard labor produced a continual supply of relatively fresh water, theirs for the dipping.

As the weeks passed, each man became more adept to the trapping of birds and small animals for food. Shellfish and fish were as abundant as one could ask of the sea with a catch acquired nearly each new day. Food then, was not the problem that it had been in the beginnings, and this employment put worthy use to their empty time so that it became most satisfying.

The men's clothing especially, seemed to be Diarmaid's next assignment for it was frayed and tattered. The daytime sun now grew very warm, and while during the cool nights the large tree leaves woven into coverlets were enough to keep them comfortable, he suspected there could come a season, even on this temperate shore, when they might need warm clothes to keep their bodies from cold and wind. He had seen small deer in the forest, and although he had not yet tried to snare one, he judged their skins would be the best covering for warmth. They were so much like the animals in the hills of his homeland that he felt certain with a bit of ingenuity, he would take a few for the purpose; deer meat would be a pleasant change in the diet as the consequence.

That evening as the six survivors participated in their customary circle after the evening meal, Diarmaid declared his hunting expedition for the next morning, and then spoke of planning a more durable shelter to be started promptly, as the eventual cooler weather must be only months away.

The Spaniards did not seem pleased with the talk of such permanence. To them it appeared that some miraculous dominion was just over the horizon ready to transport the three on to their original destination, or back to Spain its self, while the two seamen and Diarmaid were convinced that the remainder of their lives were to be spent on this wooded isle in the midst of the roaring ocean.

One expedition, only the week before, had given them notice that this piece of land on which they existed was but seven miles wide at its greatest part with placid sound style waters on that other shore. The three sailors had made this discovery and one other which they had not shared with their Spanish companions. The three agreed they detected sure sign of human life, owing to piles of open shells found in huge mounds on that other shoreline, and a judgment that divergent eyes observed them as they made their way through the undergrowth. They had encountered no mortal, village or dwelling, but Hans, Jochim and Diarmaid all concurred in a curious sensation that they were definitely not alone.

It was Diarmaid who proposed that they soon think of transporting more permanent quarters to this section of land, for its quieter and calmer nature would be more receptive to the cultivation of food with its protected refuge.

******

Estrella lay languidly at rest in the shade of the lean-to as Diarmaid approached with evening firewood. Vigilante Maria, just within speech, sat weaving a leaf coverlet. The younger woman had spoken only a trifling in the intervening weeks, continuously pouting and throwing her thick black hair willfully over her shoulders in a defiant mannerism while placing an exquisite profile up toward the sky in the attitude of haughtiness. Diarmaid thought she had little to be lofty about, as they all shared the same food, fortune, and fate, but he accepted her willfulness as plainly a sign of her upbringing and youth... although, in fact, she was six years his senior.

One night the group had played the trivial game of attempting to convey their ages to one another, despite the language barrier, and thereby established that the cousins were forty-eight and forty-five years old, the suave Spaniard was forty-two, Estrella had just reached her twenty-fifth birthday aboard the vessel, now sunk, and although protector Maria was reluctant in divulging her exact age, by discreet entreaty, they now knew her to be over forty years old. Diarmaid was spirited in claiming his nineteen years, notwithstanding the fact that he divulged he was orphaned, and his exact date of birth hidden even to himself. He also proclaimed that Bran was a healthy two year-old wolf-dog, neatly perfecting the colony.

Summer Has Come

"¡Mira, el colibri en la madreselva!" Now Estrella was sitting bolt upright and gazing into the huge oak directly before them.

Maria seemed mildly concerned with her ward's sudden emotion, yet she hardly looked up to the impulsive flurry of words so unlike the character of a sullen, unresponsive Estrella of these last months, however it made Diarmaid peer keenly into the woods before him to try to discern why she was so impassioned.

Again, "¡Mira, el colibri en la madreselva!" and she pointed to the exquisite small creature; a hummingbird, flitting from one glorious yellow blossom to the next of the huge flowers on the stout vine entwining the large oak.

The bird, intent only upon its inborn mission, did not react to her outburst, but simply pulled pleasure and nectar from each blossom, fluttering its wings furiously.

Startled at the rare outcry, Diarmaid had not seen Estrella as expressive since the wine barrel had been found on that first day of survival, and he gazed with surprise on the face of a serene, gratified, almost joyous woman, so long private. All at once, the beautiful humming creature was on, up, and over the treetops, lost to sight, yet Estrella's words came to his mind as plainly as if he fully understood her language. "Hummingbird, look, in the honeysuckle."

It was the following day as Diarmaid trampled through the green thick forest, a contented Bran by his side in search of the elusive deer, that thoughts of the former day came vividly to mind. He could not remember being this pleased within his heart since perhaps those days when he sat at the feet of those revered monks as an orphaned child in their immaculate, verdant garden. Everything seemed appealing to him: the sun filtering through leafy trees, the small animals darting before him, even the soft sea breeze filling his nostrils with its salty vapors. He stopped and stood transfigured, remembering the song of summer he had learned at the monk's knees in his Irish homeland and his brain would not abandon the beautiful words:

Behold the hope of Summer

When twigs in green appear,
When dear leap over tree stumps
and the path of seals is clear.
When cuckoo sings her gentle song
and all is peaceful, calm,
When brilliant bird skips up a hill
And breezes send their balm.

Life bursts here in every herb.
The gray stag seeks his own.
Summer is come, winter is gone.
The carefree spell is known.

Now twisted holly wounds the hound,
The blackbird sings his strain.
This year's live wood is the heritage
he may not see again.
And sunshine smiles o'er every bush,
On each soul it shines as one.
There is parting from a world of care.
Stags tryst, fish leap...
    for the Summer now has come.

He moved forward once more, his heart seeming to grow in girth with every stride of his foot on the pine straw so he at once felt that portion of every man who had eternally experienced the bountiful season. He felt neither alone nor foresaken from his own culture, and for the first time since arriving on this island, he perfected a peace that was total and good.

New Companions

Where the group, this circle of dark brown, powerful lean bodies with guarded, composed faces, had come from, Diarmaid had no understanding. It was just moments after he had cleanly killed the fleet, small deer with the new bow he had fashioned, and after Bran flushed it from behind a spruce, that he found himself quickly and totally encircled by this band of potent mighty men. He knew no fear, on the contrary, the suspicion which he held for so many weeks of other humans on this strip of land set in a wild ocean was now appeased. He keenly found his impression had been accurate and it gave him strength.

Time seemed to stand still; an eternity passed as the seven people, naked, save for their loins covered with the same type deerskin that lay on the ground amid the circle before them, showed not the slightest stir of expression or utterance from their smooth faces. Ultimately Diarmaid concluded they expected him to be the first to make a movement.

Bran too, seeming to detect a tense situation, remained alert at his master's side, unmoving. What attitude of friendship could be offered to make them know he was not combative, but wished to be their friend? Diarmaid considered a smile to be the best he might offer, so with painstaking slowness, he placed the bow aside a tree, offered his hand to the stalwart man immediately before him and smiling his broadest, most natural Irish grin, broke the tense, indolent spell.

The remainder of that memorable day moved rapidly. Pleased with his stated offer of amity, the band of natives, as one person, clustered round him, exploring Diarmaid's clothing, his blonde hair, blue eyes and the dog, Bran, who held up admirably to thorough inspection. It was made clear that they wished the tall Irishman and his wolfhound to accompany them. One of the younger men hoisted the deer effortlessly upon his broad shoulders, and they all moved through the dense forest at a rapid pace.

They arrived at the sound side of the island very near the place Diarmaid, Hans and Jochim had explored only weeks before. There, protected by a stand of heavy trees, an entire village unfolded before Diarmaid's eyes, with oblong shaped structures carefully laid out in pattern, and adjacent large garden plots clearly visible. Additionally, robust activity happened all about the hamlet. How could they have missed such a bustling, thriving area when they explored? Yet, it stood on a portion of higher ground and was completely encircled by the ring of thick evergreens. He noted the comparative serenity of its populace for a settlement of such size. It held fourteen long, loaf shaped lodgings, with one dominant lodge standing nearly at its center and yet another larger building with no visible openings, set apart at the far end of the community.

Diarmaid saw young children and women working at domestic skills or playing games alongside companions. Several women cultivated crops in the neatly marked areas and stared his way curiously as he passed them. The band of men strode straight to the core of the village where a large square platform stood. Placing the deer upon it, they showed their intentions to butcher the beast and looked for Diarmaid's agreement. He thought this a small price to pay for their friendship and nodded to tell them so. How swift and sure were the two young men who skinned the animal and cut its parts into usable meat; these they wrapped in large leaves, placing all in a huge woven basket. The skin was transported to the far end of the village where it was stretched on a frame and the two young men proceeded to scrape it with sharp shells, there to be dried in full sunlight. Diarmaid watched each act with fascination.

Truly, this was an effectual, purposeful, working community with nothing wasted, and sustaining good natured citizens. Their degree of achievement seemed to him incredible. He has heard sagas told by returning explorers of this new land and its industrious people, but he had discounted half of all they said as wild and boastful in exaggeration. Yet, what he witnessed here was a society far beyond any he might have imagined on this strip of sandy earth set in the turbulent sea.

Once the deer was disposed of, he was led into the long house that stood just off center of the village. Here they were joined by nine more men, making seventeen in all. Encouraged to bring Bran inside, they sat on woven mats placed over the dirt floor in a huge semicircle with Diarmaid and the dog at its core. Women came forward bearing hewn wooden bowls filled with a food he had never tasted. It was yellow in color, the consistency of his familiar cooked oats and had a fine, full pleasing flavor. Once finished, women again appeared bearing trays of large green grapes and dark red berries. These the men passed to one another in a ritual fashion. Diarmaid tried a piece of each food offered, and although the grape-like fruit was sour to his taste making his lips pucker, the red berries seemed honey sweet and most agreeable.

Once the empty vessels were removed, long thin pipes were taken from their places on the wall of the abode and were filled with a dark rough cut substance, then lit with the fire. In so doing, the men all sat back seemingly savoring the dense clouds of dark smoke rising from these receptacles and filling the entire building. Diarmaid had never tried this form of diversion, although he knew it to be used in the countries of Europe. Despite being overwhelmed by the smoke, odor and fumes, he cheerfully joined in the spectacle as a portion of the fellowship.

Now and then one or two of the men would rise and come to him, examining the fine bearing of Bran who stood unflinching beside his master, or then touching the blonde hair of Diarmaid as they stared deeply into his azure blue eyes with a degree of wonder.

How cordial and uninhibited they were in their manner, for here, to his delight, he found a curiosity and pureness that he would be hard put to duplicate in his own homeland.

The Larger Family

Moving from one shore of the island to the other was accomplished easy enough, for the few small contrivances the band had fashioned in the past two months for utility and comfort were easily carried by the men in the party of six. The walk was long, however, and though Diarmaid, Hans, and Jochim had traveled it twice over, clearing brush and making the path as smooth as possible for the ladies, it still was exhausting for them.

It had been a dramatic evening on that day when Diarmaid arrived back at camp with the basket of deer meat over his arm; for the natives did implore him to take his reward away, despite his belief otherwise. It then was in a mood of celebration that he unwrapped the treasure, began the cook fire, all the while excitedly attempting to communicate his astounding discovery to his own little band.

At first the revelation of foreign people and a village encamped only seven miles away was taken with great alarm by Estrella and Maria, especially, and even the count expressed caution when it came to the thought of this strange breed of humans of which Diarmaid spoke, yet he reasoned, as did the other men, the benefits of a life in an organized community must certainly take preference over this life of uncertainty.

"You must tell me more of the savages". Estrella was trying to make her words very clear. She was troubled and apprehensive. They were nearing the encampment, Diarmaid walking directly behind her.

The word savage offended his ears, yet he answered. "Offering us shelter and a share of their food, Estrella, how can you oppose such kindness ... for our survival in this land, we shall need help, and it will be good to be among other human beings."

He could not be certain that she understood all he spoke, yet she did feel the calmness of his tone and the sureness of his movement with each step as they pressed on toward the soundside shore.

Count Pedro, verbally grumbled, knowing this meant a certain end to the signal fires that he continued to build each evening, alternating his speech with the admission that these fires were probably useless anyway and his duty had ended as affairs were taken from his hands. Diarmaid felt he was secretly happily relieved of the entire burdensome situation.

Four men of the tribe came to meet the group as they reached a clearing in the tangled brush and were nearing the village. Diarmaid felt the distinct sensation that their little party was followed and watched from the very onset of the journey, but he said nothing to alert his comrades, for to him it seemed entirely natural that these people should be as curious and cautious of them as they were of the natives.

Shadows

The night truly sparkled with one million eyes, thought Estrella, lying on the platform assigned to her in a dwelling of the tribe. Maria was in a deep sleep only feet away on another pallet, plainly exhausted from their trek through the woodlands, while the young maid could look up into the heavens from between the grass matting comprising its roof, viewing a discernible ebony sky with multifarious twinkling stars above her. Now, with the actuality of being a part of the colony, her worst fears had abated to some measure. They had been treated as guests for this first day: and Diarmaid was correct, the natives seemed like small children in their delight of investigation. Her own long hair had been admired and prized, her golden jewelry fingered, and the regal mannerism to which she was so accustomed in Spain seemed recurrent. How she did enjoy being petted and pampered. Perhaps this life among these untamed people was not to be as repulsive as she at first imagined. With some sighs of resignation and a warm hand to her dark brow she turned on her side and fell into dreamless sleep.

Diarmaid, just feet away in the next small lodging, lay thoughtful too, but he, of the long life before him. So many mysteries yet to unravel in the days to come. Today, he had in manner surrendered the leadership of his small band to the ultimate fate of these stalwart peoples all about him. He must now concede his own destiny, yet hold his manner serene, just as the gentle brothers had endlessly taught him as a child; then he, likewise, was overcome by slumber.

Dawn came, then another and yet another. Each of these immigrant beings found their own way among the brown men.

Diarmaid and his sailor friends discovered that by joining with the men of the village in their pursuits of hunting and fishing, which they began just after daybreak, they were given satisfaction in real effort and the argument for existing. Sometimes the count would tag along, but on most days he wandered off alone, only to reappear in time for the evening meal. Thus the men at least, endeavored to immerse themselves into the life of the peaceful natives.

By the fourth day in camp, this was not so with Estrella. She found time heavily burdensome, unsure of any activity with which she might console herself. By this day, the village women had filled their curiosity of her identity and now went on about their own duties with scarcely a notice of her. Maria seemed no help, but clearly took her every cue from the transient whims of Estrella. Maria sat quietly in the corner of the lodge on a mat near its door, endlessly weaving the palmetto leaf into overlay, a skill to which she was now firmly adept and one that began to infuriate Estrella, in the extreme.

"Old woman, can you think of no other way to engage your time?"

It was a brutal outburst. Estrella stood above the surprised woman, hands on hips, an ugly expression emanating from her dark face. She kicked at the dirt floor near her feet, then turning on her heel without waiting for an answer, entered the lodge and threw herself flatly upon her couch although it was barely mid-morning.

Maria rose from her place and came after her with a soothing, calming tone. "Please try to content yourself, dear Estrella. Something will alter your monotony, and we shall find our way to our countrymen once more. Do be tolerant of our circumstances, for we cannot change them by anything we do."

At which, the willful Estrella only turned her dark, cloudy face to the wall and pouted all the more.

******

By the account to which Diarmaid remained faithful on his piece of parchment, the days of September were now at hand. The refugees had remained portion of this land for over six months time, although to some of them it obviously seemed a lifetime, he speculated.

It was on a day just after the midday meal, when he sat out of the warm sun on a mound of pine straw under the cooling trees in full view of the compound, thinking of how he enjoyed an idyllic, satisfied existence. The young braves of the tribe had offered him friendship, and he wanted for nothing, except perhaps only for the books to which his former life had made him accustomed.

The worst of the hot summer was ending and a cool breeze brushed his temples. This morning's hunt had been especially rewarding with two fine deer, a fat raccoon, and a host of small game in squirrels and rabbits secured for the coming winter. This land was clearly bountiful in its resources. How people elsewhere confounded their existence in the search of coin and goods when such unadorned life could be this rewarding was his continuous bewilderment.

As he sat in this reverie, his thoughts strayed to women, young women, and the fact that he had not taken his pick of the girls that he viewed in Belgium or the Netherlands, only one year ago when he was hard at work helping the monks with the Louvain translations, but at that time he gave no thought concerning any fair damsel. He felt he had years before him in which to explore their realm. Today his limited choices were the plump maidens of this tribe or the sulking, spoiled Estrella, a thought he could not easily dwell upon.

In time spent here, the routine was so predictable that it rarely varied, yet today as he sat surveying the entire village from his vantage point, he became aware of a real variance, an undeniable stirring among its people. The women moved briskly from one lodge to another, carrying vessels and bundles; likewise, a group of men busily marked some sort of path in the center field about which the dwellings were clustered.

Diarmaid rose to his full long height, and Bran alert in this move stood expectantly alongside. The activity in the village aroused his curiosity and he strode in giant steps down to its center to try and find out its purpose.

Estrella too, for all of her lethargy, felt today was finally an alteration from the usual. She had passed the lodge of the maidens on her way to the sound waters this morning for her customary immersion into its cool depths, only to glimpse a flurry of activity as each girl painted on the skin of the other, in lush color, some design making intricate, fanciful markings to completely cover their bodies.

These were the times when she wished that she could speak their languages, for the novel activity excited her curiosity. Each plump maiden seemed so happy in this childish pleasure that her jealousy was all consuming, for she had actually suffered a colorless childhood in the halls of the king's court, despite the degree to which she deluded herself to remember merriment and festive splendor. Hers were lonely days with no sister or confidant to share the cycle and only the quiet copy work, needlecrafts, and her painting classes to compel her lonely hours. Certain, the court with all its wealth and alluring trappings was majestic, but as a child she had never found herself content even to the extent that these primitive savages could giggle and savor in their simple pleasures.

The time spent in waiting was at least diverting this evening as Estrella and Maria peered from the door of their lodge at the carnival atmosphere taking over the entire camp. Strangely, the evening meal had not been served this night, and they suffered with hunger as well as the pain of curiosity, yet the flurry of movement kept them spellbound.

Finally, Hans, Jochim, Count Pedro and Diarmaid were urged from their hogan to come and sit at the very center of the festivity along with the men of the tribe. Darkness had finally fallen and torches were lighted all about the compound by a single brave in ritual fashion. Only the men were seated in the heart of the ceremony with no women to be seen. Suddenly, as by some mysterious signal, a line of maidens came forward from their lodge making their way to the path formed on the outer circle of the gathering, spacing themselves evenly about the halo.

As the two women watched, near secreting themselves, yet not reasoning why, they saw the young girls begin to perform a dance of kind, whirling and twisting to the beating of the gourds held in their hands, all tied with brightly colored cords. In a sensuous, appealing manner each young body moved and pleaded with the broad sky and the full moon above them.

The men took no part, but appraised and seemingly drew great pleasure from the shimmer of the spectacle. The twirling, swooping low, sometimes fever pitch of the maidens held the complete attention of the spectators as all eyes were bonded to the circle. Diarmaid, the seamen and the count were completely fascinated by the rhythm and agility that these formerly docile, subservient young women mounted, witnessing it from the very center of the scene.

As the dance progressed, it became evident a certain homage or fidelity was being offered to some higher deity by the uplifting movements of the maidens, and Diarmaid's intellect told him this must be some tribute of thanks for the bountiful harvest of summer crops. He noted that several of the girls filled a huge basket with portion of every type of produce grown about the compound and in doing so made particular devotion to the container.

The magnificent celebration continued for perhaps two entire hours, the maidens showing no sign of fatigue were apparently mesmerized by the repetitive flurry of their faithfulness to some higher reward.

It all ended as suddenly and abruptly as it had begun, for as by some signal, not discernible to the newcomers, the dance finished when the girls dropped to their knees in one accord and all fell silent. The shadows of their forms in the full moonlight were the only perceptible remnant of the lavish spectacle as the onlookers felt a mild sorrow at its conclusion. Brashly, the silence was broken when all the braves and old men rose as one body to form an even tighter circle, and women appeared from every hogan bearing platters of sumptuous fare. The feast lasted until the moon faded in the western sky. There was so much gaiety and laughter that Diarmaid likened it to the grand fairs and festivals he attended in the land of his birth. These natives had all the soul and disposition of any of his counterpart in that other world across the ocean and perhaps more, and he affirmed to his own joyful being that he admired, and found a warm enchantment here, he could not earlier recall.

A Jaundiced Eye

Estrella lay sleepless on the bed in her shelter. The sun was just beginning to spear mellow rays between the fronds of the side wall. She had been awake for nearly twenty-four hours, as had the entire populace of the now finally quiet village, and she should be as deep into blissful sleep as they. The pleasantry of the last night should have left her merry with its exultant diversion from the boring past weeks, however, her mood was only one of bitterness, resentment and rancor. She knew that her face held an ugly scowl, as she felt herself grinding her teeth as she had the habit of doing in her youth when she did not receive her own way.

The festival had been indulgent, assuredly, with the luscious food and entertainment, yet why did she feel so annoyed, so nettled and yes, even vengeful. The face of Diarmaid, sitting there in the center of the carnival, so friendly, so guileless, enjoying the fellowship of these infidels to such degree, made her stomach weak. Yet, why should she care? Why should she anguish over this foolish. tall foreigner into whose world her lot had been cast? What did it matter that he seemed to approve so these painted maidens with their straight dark hair and plump forms? Was she not betrothed to one of the most important men of this hemisphere? She was very sure that the governor of Cuba was sending out his ships daily in search of his promised, cherished, adorable Estrella. Matter not, that she had never seen the man to whom she was promised, the king himself had decreed their union, and she knew him to be affluent, mannered and scholarly. Soon she would be the most important woman of his land for she knew that she would be found by his emissaries.

Yet the unhappiness did not diminish, and in the rays of the ever warming sun, her incensed resentment only grew with each degree of the temperature.

Montoac

Although Hans, Jochim, the count and Maria seemed content to accept the sumptuous feast they had attended the evening before, it was not so with our inquisitive young Irishman.

Once the village again stirred in the mid-morning following the revelry, Diarmaid sought out the overseer of this hamlet to try to receive an explanation of the meaning of the festival. Croanotoa was a stalwart, aging, craggy faced man of gentle mannerism. Diarmaid had long felt it was this chief's decision which permitted the presence of their small group to be tolerated so wholly as it was by this community.

He, Croanotoa, sat apart from the remainder of the village, in his own lodging, the full front of which parted open and welcoming to the golden sunshine. Straight and tall, he sat cross-legged, serenely puffing on his clay pipe as Diarmaid slowly lowered himself to a sitting position directly across from the calm leader, assuming an exact model of the elder, as he calmly lit the pipe given to him on arrival in the compound.

There was no hurry here as in the business and mercantile houses of the continent. Time seemed of small importance to inhabitants going about daily activities in relative tranquility. The conversation therefore progressed leisurely, for although Diarmaid's enthusiasm was great, no haste seemed imperative to his understanding.

By handily making sign regarding the fete of the previous evening, Diarmaid gained from the wise old head a sacred measure of perception. After suitable judgment, the chief arched his arm skyward, then gesturing to encompass the fruits of the season heaped in abundance about his own lodging, he uttered only one word, and to accentuate it, repeated it over several times until the sound became familiar to the Irishman's ear. "Montoac," he said very resolutely, "Montoac," raising his arm high and directly above the ancient head. Diarmaid was sure he understood; his own God in whom the monks had studiously and vigorously schooled him from the age of three in St. Columba's monastery, was analogous with the power to which this tribe had paid such radiant homage, only yesterday. Indeed, Montoac and his God were one in the same!

The calmness and peace so recently invading the life of Diarmaid suddenly took on even more ebullient light. Here in this strange land, among these attractive people, he felt that truly, his God, their Montoac, was smiling certainly, and benevolently so upon his tawny head.

❧ Hallucination

What Diarmaid felt this fall morning could only be the richest, delusive, most fantastic dream of his young life. His face burned with its fresh memory. There was an earthy, amorous, brazen presence that took over his being and one he wished to unloose, yet at the same time, recall in detail for all of its disturbing, implicit pleasure.

He was alone this morning in the lodge assigned to the four men and it was just two days following the lush festival. Bran only, stood at his side awaiting the day's commitment. His rising was later than usual. It was the custom for the four men to go their separate ways with each new day, possibly to find themselves engaged in the same pursuit later without spoken plan.

An effortless life this became by any standards of more formal society, for they did what seemed necessary only for the honor of existence. Diarmaid had made plain to Chief Croanotoa of his sincere desire to work at whatever was useful to pull his weight here in the village. He, in no way, desired to add a burden to the welfare of these people, yet Croanotoa was adamant in his manner, declaring the six added souls did nothing to deplete their abundant stores and he, Diarmaid, might join in with the braves, or be free to do whatever he pleased during his life here among them, for as chief he put no demand upon those who were not of his tribe.

This morning, Diarmaid wished he had risen early in search of the roaming deer or had journeyed across the thick forest, on to the roaring surf, perchance to catch fish upon the new tide. For in so doing he would not have been captive to these troublesome images. The dream was so crystalline, the woman so known; he winced as he thought of the vision unfolding again in his mind.

She had come to him all sweet and perfumed. She had knelt at his side as he lay helpless on his pallet. His arms were leaden at his sides, and his mouth could utter no sound. Her long dark hair had essentially covered the wanton face and her breathing was husky and difficult.

Time seemed extended, as though it was a endless ribbon streaming out over miles of stones. He was incapable of even moving his eyes from her shadowed form for she held him completely under her influence. He wished to call to Bran to chase the apparition from him, but even this familiar summons was impossible. Finally, after what seemed an eternity, she pressed a kiss on his lips and a smothering impression invaded his entire form. Gasping with the sense of a drowning sensation, he attempted to throw her off, to free himself, but she endured for time that seemed infinite, only to elevate herself suddenly and smite him a vigorous blow on the side of his cheek, scratching her nails deeply into his soft flesh as she moved upward and away into the inky night. He had not wakened then, he was sure, but lapsed into yet another fancy of chained subservience in some dark tower of consciousness with this same woman his captor, unable to will any end to this persistent plight, for it seemed as though some curse, some manner of sleepspell had been cast over him, rendering him helpless, by whom he could only imagine.

Now with the morning and the bold sunlight all about him, he could not understand this uncontrolled happening in his life, nor his lack of mastery over such shameless behavior. Then reaching to smooth his mussed and tousled head, he brushed the cheek of his dream. It seemed strangely sore and to his extreme consternation, he appraised that it was cut and covered with his own dried blood.

Erotica

Estrella brought herself by way of the circular tree-lined path on this day's walk to the sheltered sound-shore where she bathed daily, savoring its waters in the caress of her own young body. She wished not to hasten the procedure this morning, but somehow linger on in her remembrance. The voluptuous sway of her gait was altogether arousing, should any person view this gorgeous, graceful creature moving with such haughty, certain bearing.

Her exploit of the previous night was to be savored, to be dwelt on for her own exquisite pleasure. Now, she had accomplished her way with the Irish fellow, he so enraptured and ecstatic during the festival as he viewed those savage maidens. She was again mistress of her own nature and intellect as well as her fine body.

No one knew or would ever know of her less than celibate behavior, least of all the ridiculous young Diarmaid, and he should never discover who had come to disturb his repose at midnight. Yes, now the spell was cast.

Hers was a mind cool and concealed from all inferior beings. She dropped her gown and dove deeply into the cleansing, cool waters.

Part II

The Book of the Lays of Fionn

The "Book of the Lays of Fionn" was compiled at Louvain in 1626-1627 by three different scribes from earlier manuscripts. The work was undertaken at the direction of Captain Somhairle MacDonnell, who was probably serving in the Netherlands at that time. The manuscript is preserved in the Franciscan Library, Dublin. Sleep Song is one poem from this collection (Duanaire Finn). It dates from the sixteenth century.

Matrimony

"I shall marry the maiden and no one will dissuade me!" The heavy figure of Jochim was standing flat footed, square in the middle of the lodge. He would give no ground to his cousin, Hans, directly before him.

The count and Diarmaid reposed in the far end of the dimly lit hogan, taking in the spirited repartee of the relatives with relish. The four had just returned from a tasty evening meal of venison and corn, and it was with this precise sunset that Jochim chose to disclose his intended wedlock.

"What then, if a ship should come to take you home to your family and friends across the ocean. Will you leave the native bride and come along?

Hans was irritated, red faced, and shaking his finger in his cousin's face.

"I assuredly would not give my vow only to break it. No, I shall remain here and put down roots. Is it that you find the color of Mineva's skin not to your liking, Hans? Surely she is as worthy and loving as any maid I should find on the European continent. I intend to stay here and raise a family, God willing, and live out the remainder of my days in contentment."

Diarmaid had not been oblivious of the hidden attention which Jochim was giving to the maiden, Mineva in these last months, ever since the dance of thanksgiving for the harvest. She had appeared then as sensous as any of the lovely maids.

Yes, there had been much lionizing and admiration between the two, for she was an abundant, buxom miss, evidently ripe for the picking. Chief Croanatoa had given his permission and the maiden her's, now the only delay was their wait for the full moon when the ritual of fidelity could be accomplished.

The festive night was soon upon them. Diarmaid admired the felicitously short ceremony bonding the two before an entire populace. It was a smiling, welcoming chief who brought the Dutchman into his fold by placing his blessing on Jochim and a giggling Mineva. Then the entire company shared a sumptuous feast and the two were escorted to a newly built hogan, just before the full moon left the western sky.

Mineva was plainly well pleased with her paunchy prize as she lead their way, and the union was smoothly accomplished.

How many moons might it be, mused Diarmaid, before his other lodge brothers would be so tempted by some beguiling female and a full moon to succumb in like manner? The connubial gods were smiling down in grand measure on this feast of harvest and it gave vent to submerged feelings that Diarmaid himself had long kept hidden.

It was only a few days later that Count Pedro and Diarmaid, by his insistence, took a walk into the verdant forest on a path not before travelled by the pair, in a discussion of troubling concerns on the Irish lad's mind.

He purposely chose this cultured, courtier, despite his forbidding manner, to speak with of issues distressing him. Diarmaid felt the count to be a discreet spirit, despite his sometime clandestine actions, for he was scholarly and thoughtful to most observation.

They chose a path which bordered the sound, blessed in unusual peace and tranquillity. Here, in the early morn, the birds at the shore swooped and stole their morning sustenance from its shining waters. Here too, a small glade was gently hidden, revealing a perfect site for words that Diarmaid wished no other to hear. He lowered his long form unto a fallen tree and asked Count Pedro to sit beside him.

"I asked you to hear me out this morning, dear Pedro, as I have need to tell someone the story of myself in hope that in the telling I will ease some of my distress. I know that I have been notably silent in the matter of my early years, whereas all of our companions have been most forthcoming.

I tell you this story today because it comes out of a pain existing in my nature. As I once did tell you, I was orphaned so early that I have no recollection of any parents. It is for this reason, when being brought up by the good brothers of the monastery, though they were wonderful to me, I suffered the strain of never knowing the female of the species; neither mother nor sister, thus ever feeling awkward in a women's presence."

By now the Spaniard was comprehending most words of the other languages of his fellow refugees and the count conceded that he understood all Diarmaid spoke by a nod of his head. He felt much like father-confessor to this young, good looking Irish lad, who was but half his own age, yet he was reasonably honored too that he should be taken into his confidence.

"We had a good life there in the abbey of St. Columba. The monks were wonderfully kind to me and indulgent too, as I was the only youth in the monastery. They taught me both religious and secular treatises, and it was my belief that one day I would probably join them to become a godly man and live there too, for it seemed small recompense to honor these devout persons who had provided me life?

Yet, something bizarre happened to change my life a few years before I ventured upon the trip forcing me here. It is this pitiable occurrence that causes me to speak to you today.

When I was just fifteen years old, the good brothers entrusted me with the mission of purchasing supplies from the nearest town to our abbey. This was some sixteen miles distant and in so doing they gave me both a burro and dog to accompany me. It was an exciting task, done once with each season. The first, a winter trip had gone well, despite a driving, cold rain, and the spring excursion was a miracle of wonder with the grandeur of new life bursting all about me. It was in the summer journey I found the deplorable restriction to which I must speak.

The kind monks had arranged a respite, a stop, at the home of a Mr. Groton, a merchant, living just outside the village. Since half of the trip took one full day they bargained this stay-over in his outer building for myself and the animals.

I had watered and fed both donkey and dog and was standing in the doorway of the shelter eating the bread and cheese I purchased in town for my supper, when I heard my name called, at first so softly, I could not be sure of its certainty and then more clearly until I realized that Dame Groton stood in the doorway of her home not twenty paces distant and beckoned to me. I can still remember the full moon casting an ominous glow upon that scene with the summer roses twining all about the doorway and the heavy smell of them lingering on her shiny brown hair as I entered her door.

It seemed Mr. Groton was in Dublin on his seasonal buying trip, and she bade me sit and have supper with her as she said she was lonely and could use the agreeable company. The sweet vegetable soup was praiseworthy, the biscuits fine, and it at once seemed as though I was enjoying the pleasures a mother might have brought to me. She explained that she never had the tender love of children and sorely missed this singular blessing.

Evelyn, for she bade me call her by her Christian name, was a rounded pleasing woman, insisting I take the spare room for my night's rest in place of the hay loft, and so it was decided.

It must have been about midnight that a most curious event happened. The full moon was lighting my small cubicle with pale luster when I sensed a figure full above me as I lay on the narrow cot. Her long perfumed hair swept across my bare chest, covering me with goose flesh as it brushed over my skin. I felt as though it was a dream, for the illusion was so foreign, so forbidding. The figure placed her body upon mine and I was, or pretended to remain asleep, I know not which, should this not be the fantasy I hoped it was. Yet the essence of the hair near stifled me with its oppressive scent and the weight of her form was real upon my own. Her breathing was hoarse and uneven and to this day I can wake to hear that sound. I lay rigid, frozen to the pallet as my mind could not function with any clarity. I cannot say how many moments or hours this state endured, yet the first rays of the morning light were entering the room when I at last found her gone. My clothing lay in a heap upon the floor at the foot of the cot and my body ached with anomalous sensation. I shall never know what really happened on that night, for I dressed immediately, slipped out of the house, led my burro from the stable and in moments was on the road to the abbey.

You must understand, mine was a sacred mission. Had I not carried costly goods for the charitable brothers, which they sorely needed, I believe I should, on that very day, departed Ireland to find a fresh life far from that place.

It is an episode I have not revealed to any living soul and one I still have trouble understanding, still I came to the decision that in the telling, I might rid myself of the panic I yet sense in its remembrance. It is strange, for I almost thought I had lost this shame and apprehension where it applies to the female gender, then only two months ago, a peculiar dream came to me in the lodge. It was that of another woman above me in the midst of the night and this time she struck me a blow and was gone.

Can you detect what significance this has? Am I to endure life never knowing the love and warmth of a tender, gracious woman? The marriage of Jochim is what started me thinking again of this old pain. I want to be lover to a damsel one day, yet until I can rid myself of this curse in memory ever connected with sleep, I cannot be a whole man."

The story was finished. Count Pedro understood the implications of this trauma into which a fifteen year old boy was placed. Had not he himself, gloried in the ladies of the court of Spain at this same age, yet he did not suffer such humiliation, having grown up with sisters and the sweet love of a gentle mother. His was fond remembrance and he would not exchange those youthful memories at court for any offered gold. How then could he convince this fresh young man that the wide world did hold the adoring woman for him, and this was but a minute lesson in the eccentric ways of females and of life.

The day, approaching its mid-mark with the lush glade all encompassing, was warming to the noon sun. The birds had ceased their frantic flights in search of live food and were calmly pecking the shore for infinitesimal insects to fill their avaricious bellies.

The companions fell silent for a time, merely watching this singular portion of nature, quite content to be at ease as one with the elements. Then Pedro broke silence with what words he deemed judicious for the occasion.

"I, who have neither son nor brother, am possibly not the best of counselors, nor do I believe this is essentially what you need. However, dear Diarmaid, do consider this ancient incident for what it truly is, merely a portion of the circumstance we are all placed in at some time of our existence. Do not labor over what has gone before, but put it behind you to know that as creatures here on earth we are weak and some of us to a greater degree than others. Do not condemn that pitiful woman from the past, for we do not know to what degree she may have been tempted, or if she had the knowledge of how her indelicate transgression could wound your spirit, even here, nearly five years hence.

As to the dream, we all recall in our repose some inconsistencies of the past. As evidence, I will tell you that I dream of the boat's overthrow and our crashing on this shore, perhaps once in every month, yet to dwell upon it would be foolhardy, for it fades as quickly as the daylight if we permit it. No, let these memories decline now as fragment of your fledgling days and go on to pursue those things you wish to with no turning backward, even to the employment of wooing a maiden, should that be your heartfelt yearning."

Bran, who had been lying quietly at his master's side for all the warm morning, stretched out long and then stood eager to chase the birds still energized on the shore. It seemed to the two men this was signal of consummation to these revelations of the soul and they too rose to their feet.

"Thank you, dear Pedro for listening to this prattle. I do feel better for the telling, and I trust this tale never be told beyond this forest."

"You have my word, dear Diarmaid."

Wild Steeds
Garran

Boredom hung on Estrella as though one could visibly view the weight. Her body lost that once fiery spirit, and even her voice, although seldom heard, suspended its brilliance.

Her days were so much the same, she scarce could remember the former and she spent most of her time on her bed, pining for fortune lost.

The occasions of the few festivals were the only diversity, and now even these were beginning to lose their fascination for the girl. Equally, her degree of jealousy seemed diminished and Maria was greatly concerned for her well being. If only some sport, some pleasure were introduced, perhaps the girl could catch on, take interest, but what prospect did they have in this tedious existence.

By this date, the gentle, temperate days were about at an end and the cool winds of winter, upon them all. While the men seemed encouraged by the season's vigor, the women stayed inside the hogan all the more and grew pale and wan. Not so with the native women who found countless tasks, industriously filling each hour of their day.

The three in the men's lodging, along with the bearded bridegroom, joined the young braves in the interesting employment of fashioning new dugout canoes during these cool months, making ready for the new season, all the while continuing to fish and hunt daily for the needs of the hamlet. And so it was a doubly busy time for them and they exalted in the rewarding task of seeing real goods as a result of their labors.

These long, narrow canoes, so amazingly built without the use of metal instruments, truly awed the Europeans. The canoes varied in size with some as large as to carry twenty men and chests, yet all were light weight in contrast to the vessels known to the newcomers.

Each boat was constructed from its own log, carefully chosen from the swampy forest. It looked to Diarmaid like a kind of white cedar, for he knew this wood and its resistance to rot. The natives called the trees, "Rakiocke," and they seemed to show great reverence for its height and strength.

After what seemed to the novices suitable lessons in watching the native industry for a week or so, the brown men permitted each of them to try their hand at helping in the strange procedure. After the right tree was selected, the braves built a fire at the root with moss and chips of wood that was perfectly controlled by one man at its base. This process was repeated over and over again for sometimes days, or until the tree fell to the ground in a selected manner which did not injure its parts. Then the men removed all boughs and finally cut through the trunk by another burning to produce the length of tree desired. They then raised the log on forked posts and scraped off bark with clam shells, finally burning out the log again to hollow it. Once into the desired shape, they placed gum and rosin all around the sides to seal it, repeating the process time and time again until it was finally finished.

Never had the foreigners seen such a display of industry, ingenuity and chiefly, patience. It made them feel deficient in the sense that here, with no tools and such minimum of material, these hardy people could produce such intrinsic product. The fact made them humble by comparison.

******

Now in the beginnings of January on a day not extremely cold, the young men of the village initiated a trip to test their newest large canoe and invited their guests to go along. It was an early start southward, across a slightly choppy inlet that they made their way. The Europeans long suspected, talked of, and envisioned a separate island to the south of their habitation, yet it had remained just an unsupported impression. Now they were to be privileged to explore yet another island, perhaps to view dissimilar peoples and peculiarities.

Although at first glance the landscape looked much the same as the shore they left, upon embarkation and a short walk down the atoll on a narrow strip of land with rumbling ocean on one side and placid sound on the other, the four white men and the six natives accompanying, came upon a village much comparable to the one they had left, except smaller in size and visually even more cultured in nature. It surrounded a sector of lake cut from the ocean, creating a most peaceful harbor for a fleet of canoes greater in size than their village possessed, despite its smaller population.

Upon inquiring of their hosts as to what name this place was called, they received the answer of "Wococon". A word strange, but one their ears would memorize. The natives and the four were welcomed with much delight and it became occasion for festivity. The strangers were touched, admired and stroked just as they tolerated when first found on Hatorask, yet it was with such dignified and esteemed behavior, that it did not displease the subjects.

One enormous curiosity was exhibited in the first hour of their visit. The entire tribe seemed fervent to reveal a recent acquisition, and one attained since the Croatan visit of only months before. Penned in a large wild growth of woodlands, immediately adjacent to their village, a herd of wild horses bolted, reared and reveled with healthy mein. Here were magnificent animals and at least twenty of them, all silken brown with manes flying. These were not docile beasts of burden but some who had plainly fought for life and won. It was clear, they were not to be easily tamed by the natives nor given to domestication, for they definitely held wills of their own and were majestic in their breed.

The enigma was instantaneous. How had these handsome equine come to this island in the midst of the ocean? It was a perplexity of considerable magnitude. The Europeans questioned among themselves while the Wococon explained it to the Croatan. Finally Pomooc, a young brave and one who was friend to Diarmaid, very probably about his own age, explained it to the group with what words he now knew and with the sign language that was becoming ever easier for the white men to comprehend.

It seemed in the December storm, or during the last moon, as the Wococon described it, a large ship was sighted close into the waters off the southern most tip of their land. They watched it through the wild, windy hours believing it was trying to make safe harbor to the refuge of their sheltered cove. Alas with the morning light, only wreckage remained where the huge vessel had been seen and then shortly after, this herd of powerful horses swan to their shore, shaking salt from their manes in happy reunion with the others. No person had been saved. The tribe insisted that their visitors view the objects that had washed ashore during those next days following the storm.

In one small lodge was stored a variety of gear, most of which the natives seemed unable to recognize. It was all too apparent to the newcomers upon examining the booty, that this had been a rich Spanish galleon by the wealth of heavy golden urns and goblets, the remnants of costly sail, and a piece of painted wood bearing the name of the vessel.

Count Pedro then was certain it was a ship headed for Cuba or another colony on this side of the ocean, but forced off course in the tempest, only to be dashed upon the shoals about this shore.

The name he read on the plank was The Concerto di Ombre with its home port, Cadiz. He wondered aloud if it could have been searching for himself and Estrella, the notion which Diarmaid believed and hoped he had finally set aside.

Gift

So now, here they were, the six mighty braves, two of whom were handling the forward direction and motion of the log craft while the other four held solidly to the thongs leading the wild, swimming horses. The Europeans sat in the midst of this sport fearing they might capsize at any moment. The horses, although willing to swim the narrow inlet, lest they drown otherwise, were not such sensible strategists, stirring the waters into great waves with their forceful mass while distressingly trying to take the light craft out to sea.

If it were not so frightening thought Diarmaid, it would be hilarious to see these ten men pulling five strong horses through the swells of the frenzied waters; for their brothers on Wococon would have nothing less than to share their good fortune with their worthy equals on Hatorask.

Miracle

No one was immune to the spectacle brought forth on that cool winter's eve as at last our weary group escorted the five wild steeds onto the outer limits of the village.

It was not as though some of the elders of the tribe had never seen such animals, for this same type of beast swam ashore in their youth, but then with no mares among them, had died off with the years. The children were the most delighted however, this was a great event with all its dramatic implication for adventure in the days ahead.

What took Diarmaid's eye, tired and bone sore though he was, was the manner in which Estrella stood just gazing at the creatures with wide, sparkling eyes. He could only remember once before when she observed the bird in the vines, that she appeared so alive. Could it be the stimulation of nature in birds and beasts was all which moved her?

As the natives strode all about admiring the herd, shouting and excited, she stood aside in awe, somewhat as though she had just fully awakened, persuaded from some inward slumber. She neither moved her hands nor form, but watched each movement of the horses with large, appreciative childlike eyes.

It was a time impossible to hold one's tongue and Diarmaid took her side in devotion to the thunderous herd.

"In Erin we call them garran, what wild magnificent creatures; are they not?"

He put it in a manner of entreaty so that he might elicit her speech in response. There was a extended pause before she spoke, still not removing her eyes from the prancing shapes.

"I believe them to be the most magnificent creatures God has placed on earth. I thought I should never see a stallion again and it has been but one judgment which sorely grieved me. Now it is as though a miracle has occurred; I must be dreaming for here in this purgatory that has made captive of me, I believed that I should never see such beauty and grace repeated. It is truly a benediction to my soul."

Diarmaid stood staring at the anemic, petite girl, now so enraptured, she did not face him as she spoke. He had no way of knowing of her passion for these creatures. He certainly had never seen her as fervent. Could it be that God had sent these steeds to somehow break a spell of depression in this woman. He had great faith in the sureness of the Deity, yet was this not too sizable to accept, even by himself?

Pardon

The first one up and out of her lodge each day after the introduction of the wild horses was our Estrella. She appeared as a fresh person to all of the inhabitants of the town. Her first action, following the momentous night of the steeds arrival, was to go to Chief Croanatoa pleading her case for permission to try to gentle one of the herd, and if able to do so, gaining his consent that she might ride that horse whenever and wherever she would.

Pleased that she would seek the favor of his approval, the chief ordered a brave to accompany her and give her support in the daunting struggle, for struggle was what her plan became. Each morning a determined Estrella would march to the enclosure where the horses were kept. First she remained on the outside of the barrier, attempting to entreat the beasts to come to her. Usually she saved a portion of her morning corn cake with which to tempt them, and this proving finally successful on the third morning, she ventured inside the loamy tract. From the very beginning she set her mind on one horse in particular. The tallest of the stallions was a chestnut with white markings about the face. He was a beautiful creature and the one she determined to tame.

Each winter's day she spent her waking hours with the wild beasts and with each day she found a little less aggression and a wider measure of recognition. Also a curious group of observers, on the tranquil days just outside the barrier, watched her quest with awe and admiration.

Not only were the natives totally bewildered by this heretofore quiet, sullen young woman, suddenly so swift and alive, but the Europeans, her shipwrecked comrades, came to the enclosure daily to marvel at the spectacle.

She had been hard at this discipline for over two weeks and this day was particularly bitter; the north wind blowing up a gale and the horses sensing the storm. Estrella had been working with all of the horses, but especially the one she had named, "Celebrar". She had progressed to a point in the training where she managed to individually slip a noose about three of the steeds. These ceased to balk at her leading them about the pen in a circle. She felt accomplished today, for her champion, "Celebrar", had behaved in excellent fashion, allowing her to guide him about the compound for two full laps. She was cold and her hands felt the sting of the hemp as she finished, now all her thoughts were of rest in the warm lodge. Maria would be there waiting with hot sassafras tea. The old pleasantry had returned in their relationship in these last weeks with her renewed interest for living, and it was all the consequence of these gorgeous creatures.

She had just slipped under the bough which served as bottom rail and raised her raven head, when she felt a warm form standing tall beside her. The winter's light was beginning to fade and she was startled, failing to recognize someone so close.

"Diarmaid, you frightened me. I thought I was quite alone here today. It has grown so cold, my teeth chatter, I must gain my lodge."

"Could you take one moment and speak with me, Estrella? I'm astounded by your splendid style of work with the horses. You must have studied such pursuits when you lived in Spain."

And then without waiting for her answer, Diarmaid removed his woven cape to place it about her shivering shoulders. She lifted her oval face to his, now towering above her with a strange, skeptical expression. They had seemed adversaries for these long months, why now did they seem to share some common optimism? Her head was too full of the ferocity of her discipline with the steeds so that she could be taking a false meaning from his solicit manner. Warily, she pulled the covering about her shoulders.

"I must get to the hogan, I am so cold." If you wish to come with me, do so, and we can talk there."

It was the closest thing to being civil that Diarmaid had yet to envision.

"Come, then," he said, taking her arm in a genuine gesture of concern, Come along Estrella, and we will talk."

❧ *Dialogue*

That first tangible discourse between the Irish man and Spanish maid opened a myriad of interests which the two had never thought conceivable. Why, strained Diarmaid, as he lay on his couch nights later, had it taken so long to find the physical person; so many wasted hours, so many difficult seasons.

It became a tea party of sorts, when they finally reached the hogan, a cold, brisk walk from the pen of stallions. Maria registered mild surprise, finding a pair of young persons prepared to sip the brew she had waiting for her mistress alone. But then it was only one of many jolts during these last weeks as she discovered her charge to be fresh with energy. Life for herself too, took on new stature. She felt her profession of chaperone was once more honored and it gave her purpose for being.

Once tea was served, she discreetly withdrew to the rear of the dwelling, out of the hearing of this energetic woman and her new companion.

Estrella was vibrant now, her cheeks ablaze with the result of entering the warm hogan and leaving the wintry, numbing gusts. She sat on the floor of the hut as had become her custom, imitating the hosts of this village. Diarmaid, opposite in like fashion, sipped hot tea from an earthen cup. Estrella placed her familiar golden cup to her lips. It seemed ever a succor of kind; a remembrance of royal times past and a comfort in its extravagance.

What an amicable setting, thought Diarmaid. Who would ever have envisioned himself sitting across from the lovely Estrella, sharing tea, here in this simple dwelling, so far from accepted civilization, even now it seemed illusion.

"And now, can you answer my question? How is that you know so much about horses?"

Estrella took a long drink of the brew and placed it before her on the mat.

"The equine and I have much acquaintance with one another for I was raised to ride in a royal fellowship of horsewomen. It is a great discipline in my country, that children of regal station should be schooled in such artistry. We hold the horse in high esteem, applauding loudly those who master the skill. I must tell you in all modesty, that I was the paramount horsewoman in my country, the king himself riding with me on many occasions."

Now Diarmaid was seeing the true Estrella. She had lifted her image in proud attitude and was looking directly into his face with shining black eyes. Her birthright was now disclosed in every aspect of her bearing and she beamed as she spoke, unlike any essence he had ever seen in her.

"The steeds have made a marvelous difference in the way you view your life here Estrella. Are you now happy and do you think you will remain satisfied?

"Who can tell, but for now I have a mission, a task I can put my body and mind to and that is all I ask of this period. I still hold hope of our being found by some Spanish ship, for the knowledge that these horses came from the same sort of craft makes me all the more certain freedom is only a matter of time away. I shall be mistress of Cuba, and before many months, I allow!"

The flush of her face and the proud demeanor of her gorgeous head, at last seemed impossible to endure, and he had to look off into the shadowy depths of the long house to avoid her bright eyes. His senses told him that he had very potent feelings about these last words which Estrella had spoken and he must come in grasp of his own reason before any ship was to be sighted.

Fete

These late afternoon affairs were becoming a habit by the end of the winter. The horses no longer recoiled at Estrella's gentle hand as she placed it over the fence each morning at the beginnings of her exhilaration. They were nearly tame, at least notably the chestnut, and Diarmaid, despite any other activity, found himself drawn to the pen at the end of each day, relishing the prospect of viewing Estrella and her commitment.

Daily, he would wait until she completed her pattern, then they would walk to the hogan where invariably Maria would have the familiar tea prepared for two.

Their's had ultimately become a manageable relationship, Estrella having lost her lofty manner to put in its place a refined, satisfied deportment, yet fixed in Diarmaid's mind was the fury of the beasts always present between them. Diarmaid's reasoning strayed at times, even while pleasantly talking with his companion, as the possibility of the sudden absence of this diversion, which had so transformed her, might end. The image of what could occur should she lose it, sadly loomed before him. He could never be sure if his presence held the element in her shift of character, yet he dared to hope it to be so.

"Tell me about your days in the monastery, Diarmaid, I would like to hear of how your time was spent and of the monks who raised you."

They had progressed thus far in their dialogue. It was satisfying, for each afternoon one would tell the other some story of their life on the other continent. Diarmaid had learned that Estrella was the only child of a middle-aged nobleman and his young wife, both of whom were reared in the courts and knew no other existence. Hers had been a privileged life with every luxury attainable, for these were the golden years of great wealth and grandeur in Spain and no wish had been denied her. She speculated that she may have been spoiled by such affluence and could not equate with the ordinary man or woman of her day. This seemed to him a startling confession from a woman so soaring only weeks past.

"Life in the abbey was routine, simple and above all, ideally joyful," began Diarmaid. "Infrequently I think back on those times with pure languish for it was a life of supreme tranquility of soul; yet most probably not the one I was meant to enjoy, otherwise fate would not have led me here. As to the brothers who raised me, I have many splendid recollections, especially of Brother Clare and Brother Shane, for they were truly mother and father to me, teaching me manners, speech and assuredly ethics."

So saying, Diarmaid lowered his tawny head in reflection, so close that Estrella could observe the halo of curly bright hair rise from his scalp in concentric pattern and as it was brought closer to her face she felt very inclined to reach out to caress its bright strands.

"How did you happen into the Netherlands, Diarmaid, for I am sure you said that was your place of departure on that voyage which has made us all prisoners of this land."

Diarmaid had raised his head to recount the days prior to the journey. He was merry in this chronicle of his adventures.

"When I was seventeen, three of our brothers, those celebrated scribes of our order, were requested to go to Louvain in Belgium to compile The Book of the Lays of Fionn. This work was done under the direction of Captain Somhairle MacDonnell. It was to take nearly two years, and I had the honor to accompany the monks as companion and assistant in the running of errands, preparing of meals, and in general as adjunct to their needs. For other reasons, I was most eager to see more of the world than my limited view, for thus far my life was lackluster and this venture seemed particularly intriguing to a guarded lad of seventeen.

When we arrived in Louvain, we were lodged in a monastery, yet exposed to the outside world to a much greater degree than in Ireland. We lived within the gates and the bustle and exhilaration of Louvain was all about us. The Brabant is exciting with its weaver's industry, its grand Cloth Workers Hall and newly built

City Hall. There was merriment and life everywhere, even as we strove to do the work set upon. I walked freely about the streets, daily obtaining goods and information for the monks.

As you may know, the monasteries in which we made our home in Ireland were grievously outlawed by the Protestants and as there we existed in secret, here, we felt the inference of a freedom never before known.

The great curiosity in the matter of the translations on which my three friends and mentors toiled daily, was that these were the Lays or Songs of Fionn, our Irish ancestor, named Fionn mac Cumhail, probably living in the third century. One of the most famous tales speaks of Diarmaid and Grainne, his lover, as the most celebrated story of passion in our literature. The tale has been passed down for hundred's of years and it is for this luminary that the good brothers named me. It seemed strangely fateful, that I should be even a small part in their effort to translate this epic for all posterity, and for that reason, it was exciting, indeed

Bran was the name of Finn's great wolfdog, the greatest ever bred in Ancient Ireland, and thus Bran is what I made bold to name this animal given to me by the good brothers, in honor of that other splendid beast."

The pieces were coming into place now, thought Estrella. This young man, while of so much authority and power where it equated the male, due to his upbringing, was a mere novice in the hands of any damsel. Her rationale as to his true personality was now growing heady and unsure. Prior, she perceived him but a mere lad with no thought of intimate interplay, but now with his head so close, sharing his most inner thoughts, he appeared much more man than she could have believed, only weeks before.

"How then, if you were so involved with these translations, did you arrive in the Netherlands and aboard the vessel bound for this continent?"

"It becomes rather an involved story, Estrella, however when the monks were finished with the work they had set to do and the manuscripts were accomplished, I asked Captain MacDonnell if I might travel with him, for a time, back to the Netherlands where he was stationed so I might see more of the world. The monks and I parted then, myself promising to return one day to St. Columba's and my loving family of men so dedicated to God. They insisted I take our companion, Bran, along as gift and protector in the mad world beyond the safety of the monastery. I shall never really know if I did the right thing in leaving my brothers, for now I do not believe I shall ever be united with them again."

Diarmaid fell silent for a time, gazing out into the winter darkness of the camp. He seemed so considerate, so gentle when speaking of his former life, Estrella could not help but be moved in sympathy.

"Tell me the story of this Diarmaid of the ancient books. Was he much like you, sweet Diarmaid?"

He looked at her quizzically then. Did this earlier rude and vain creature say sweet in reference to himself? Could her character be so altered by her new occupation and this opening of dialogue between the two of them, or was there a hidden, more sinister motive hiding in her woman eyes? Suddenly the friendly face of Evelyn Groton took the place of Estrella, and he knew he must excuse himself for tonight, at least, to reflect on the unsullied merits of her female design.

Slight Knowledge

In the weeks following his doubts about this Spanish maid, Diarmaid decided to throw prudence to the winds, and although inexperienced in the manner of women, to merely appreciate whatever the gods sent to his direction with that same naked ignorance.

In keeping with this dictum, as the days grew more obliging and with temperate March gusts at their backs, the pair took to riding the steeds upon the wild, sandy beaches of the island; Estrella upon the horse, Celebrar, and Diarmaid upon a sorrel he called Loch Derg or Red Lake, for he said he reminded him of that rare wild place in Ireland with all of its raw spirit.

The two would meet each morning, early, just outside Estrella's lodge, to tramp to the pens and snare their particular mount. Although the horses still feigned a reckless disposition, it was plain now that they too were eager for the attention and exercise as they did not struggle over-long before their captors.

All of the mornings were spent thus, the only exception, those days too inclement to venture forth. The populace was well aware of the two young people going off together and it seemed disturbing to no one.

Estrella was radiant these days, thought the Irish man, with her hair again glossy and raven, her skin the color of ivory, and finally a deep throated laugh resounding through the green forest as they galloped along its edge.

Today, with these early days of March, the wind was of zephyr quality as the pair raced faultlessly like the very devil was at their backs. Celebrar essentially always won the impromptu contests which could be inaugurated on a single word, for he was pure champion, an invincible animal, as keen-eyed Estrella had spied from the first.

It was nearing noonday with a sea akin to silken blue satin spread out before them. Exhausted by the flurry of energy this gracious spring day had engendered as each challenged the other to yet another race, at last they slipped from their steeds as one person, breathless, to sit on soft sea moss curving over the brown tide line.

"We could be anywhere else on earth today, Estrella, and not find a scene as lovely."

Diarmaid waved his arm to encompass the magnificent land, resplendent warm winds, azure sky and bountiful sea as the setting.

"It is true, we could be the only persons on the earth as I view this spectacle. Would you like to pretend at that particular fancy, dear Diarmaid?"

Her question had the quality of saucy badgering to it, that biting small sarcasm in her tone. He sensed it immediately, yet would not fall captive to its temptation. He had given much thought to this woman who sat only inches from him now, in fact, she was probably in his mind more than any other waking admission. Was this, now, the right time to find her true feelings toward him? It seemed so with no other human to trouble them and only sky and sea to witness his own perceptive naivete.

"Yes, I should like to deceive myself in just such manner for an hour or so ... here on the sand. Do I shock your sensibilities, eh, Estrella?"

Her face shone in a savage, gratified, yet forbidding attitude, all at once. He had startled her then, for this was his intention. Too long had this woman toyed with his emotions, never conceding her own, playing with him like cat with mouse.

"It is time to admit we will occupy this reef for perhaps an eternity, Estrella. Are we to be old, bowed and greyed people before we begin to know what is in the other's heart? Since you have discovered the horses, you seem a new person to my mind. I did not like that other woman who sulked and brooded, who injured and misused her fellow men. Is it possible that I can see some future for the two of us in this place, or do I read your sentiments mistakenly?"

He had expressed his true temper precisely as he had wished to. He was satisfied with his speech. Now it was her turn to declare, to tell him just what she felt within her very core.

"I have wished to be open with you, Diarmaid, for some time now. It is very disturbing to give up all the dreams and hopes I had for the future. I was raised to believe I should be a noblewoman, in command of great wealth and domain one day. This, I was taught from the cradle and it is incredibly difficult to recognize any opposite outcome to that destiny. Can you now understand what I relinquish by becoming submissive to this "native" existence? I was to own luxury and affluence and now I am to be no more than a peasant, what would be a common servant in my homeland, yet here to become dweller in the woven lodges, a keeper of the wooden bowls, the earthen floor. Can you see why I am so wretched? I am much better than this!"

Now once more Estrella was that complaining, superior woman of the beach one year earlier. Her bosom rose and fell with raging indignation with her discourse and Diarmaid longed to witness the gentle equestrian once again. Perhaps it was too soon to try to make her understand reality. He had spoken his inner thoughts too easily. She was still living in some fantasy of mansions and servants. Would she ever become a touchable creature, realizing that those things were forever gone from her?

His back was to the shore as he pondered whether it was any further use to push this episode to understanding. His face so close to hers that he was tempted to bend ruefully over and kiss her lovely pink lips; when all at once she sat bolt upright before him and as quickly rose to her feet, pointing her arm straight out from her body toward the horizon. The sudden flurry of her movement nearly toppled his form unto the soft sand as he whirled about to see what had aroused her so savagely.

There, plainly visible on the rim of that portion where sea met sky, clearly silhouetted against a radiant blue backdrop, rode a lone galleon, sails billowing, its bow rising and falling with the cresting waves.

Diarmaid's hopes, in like tempo, rose and fell seemingly as rapidly. If this should be a ship to reach this island it meant the end to an existence he was only beginning to affirm. Yet, to Estrella it meant escape, for she was now meeting the water's edge, her feet in its surf, shouting and waving in absurd industry to make someone on the vessel aware of her identity.

Anguished

So close and so far. The ship had turned as suddenly as it appeared in that one brief moment of fervor. It was all Diarmaid could do to physically hold Estrella from thrusting her body into the waves in attempt to reach the ship. Foolhardy though she knew it to be, it seemed the one desperate act she could undertake in her travail.

Now, sobbing and dejected, she stood at last, arms at her sides, in dispirited confusion.

Diarmaid took her warm body into his arms and she did not rebuff his action. He understood her bitter disappointment and wished to soothe this woman he now felt only compassion for. Somehow he would make her see that the other world, beyond this faultless shore, was not what she believed it to be. For even now, in his youthful judgment, the fact was becoming more clear with each passing day; Magh Mell, the Plain of Honey, the invisible world on which his Celtic culture was founded, was here, existent on this island or group of islands, separated from that other shore of hate and greed by the omnipresent ocean and it was his vision and duty to bring this maiden to see Magh Mell, as clearly as he saw it today. He knew in one rush and as infallibly as he knew his God, that his eyes must have been prophetically opened under those waves when he was nearly drowned, with Bran saving him from certain death; that this was as close to a Magh Mell as he, Diarmaid of Ireland, was ever to see, and he was destined to make it his ... and Estrella's for eternity.

Persuasion

Whatever he should do and however he would act for the next lifetime of years before him, thought Diarmaid, hinged only on dialogue he would instill in this maiden in the next weeks.

The days of playful horseback rides continued. It was an unsaid condition now that with the first rays of morning light the two would meet at the pen to take their steeds for the sunrise romp.

For the most part, they raced along the seashore with wild wind nearly always penetrating the cool dawn air. It was as though time had frozen in place; the two, intent only upon the pleasure of the furious sport and the exercise it gave both body and spirit. Few days were exempt, for on this "flowery plain" the atmosphere was ever conducive to outdoor enterprise.

It was the springtime once again and all of nature sent welcoming evidence with each new morn.

Perhaps, thought Diarmaid, this particular radiant day is the moment I have waited for, but then this reasoning went through his head with each successive dawning.

It had now become habit when the horses and their riders were spent, by the mid-interlude of their bounding run, that the pair should seek the shelter of some shaded site to let the steeds cool, and likewise take their own ease. It was at these times that the two had ultimately begun to detect the others reasoning.

He felt he understood this willful woman now with all her solemn demeanor. She could not so easily give up her fanciful pleasures to become one with this foreign place; whereas he with all his recent unadorned existence, could welcome it for what he truly believed it to be, Magh Mell.

******

"Estrella, these last months have been so joyful for me. It is my hope that they have been as good and plenteous for you. I wish to broach a subject which I probably have no reasonable calling to pursue, yet if we are to live and remain together on this tract of land for the remainder of our days, I feel there is no profit in any added period of waiting to speak to you of what is in my heart."

Yes, now the breach had been opened. There was no turning back this day. He must open his soul to this maid who would not leave his mind by noon or night, and put an end once and all to the question he had.

"Remember that lone galleon that appeared on the horizon some weeks ago? The very fact that we were powerless to make our being known to the vessel, proves to me that we shall never be delivered from this appealing isle. Why should we both waste our youth and vigor waiting for something which will never happen? Do you see what I am saying, dear Estrella, why cannot we two become the lovers which fate seems to have decreed, and spend the remainder of our lives as one?"

There it was said! Diarmaid sat at the base of a live oak, staring fully into her eyes, and now scarcely could believe he had been so brazen. Those familiar phrases he said over and over during the dark night in his lodge were now exposed to the bright light of day. They could never be recalled. She now knew what he had been thinking these last months.

With burning cheeks, he sat there as time moved at an indolent pace. What could she be thinking of him now, she of regal birth and he an orphaned wanderer, as he proposed one life the two might share?

Perhaps it was the beauty of the season; possibly the peaceful breeze fluttering the budding leaves above them, or equally, the blissful sound of the waves washing upon the shore just within sight, he might never know, yet this beautiful, unique, unpredictable woman rose suddenly from the stump where she sat listening intently to all he said, to place her warm body very close to his own, occupying the soft moss beneath the tree. Her slim young arms twined about his tanned neck as she lifted a small dark face to his in plenteous submission.

"I affirm, I could be in love with you, Diarmaid, and I now give to you all that you desire of me, but only after this act shall we discern if our love is certain destiny!"

❈ True Love Asthor

It was a full fortnight later, yet Diarmaid was as captivated, as spellbound, as he had been on that fateful morning in the fragrant moss. His mind was filled only with headstrong Estrella and her diverse moods; his total being bent solely to her whims and desires and although his strong intuition fought against them, his lot seemed now cast in her considerable eccentric peculiarities.

Today would mark the first anniversary of their frantic expulsion; the six pilgrims cast onto this narrow strip of world set into its sometime wild and sometime placid ocean.

As Diarmaid awoke, from dreams too frenzied to recollect, the sky was just beginning to show a gentle light. He wondered if reference at all should be made to his fellow companions on the matter of the date. Certainly it was not one to be celebrated, although they all had been absorbed into the routine of the tribe in not such an unsavory life after all, for they were alive and healthy, their daily needs met with little difficulty and for him, the very lack of stress of the European lifestyle, even that slight portion he had lived, was altogether pure luxury.

It was impossible to declare for the others, but for himself, he was completely satisfied.

Then rolling from his pallet and standing his towering young body in stretch with the new day, he questioned if satisfied was indeed an accurate description. The endless craving which Estrella represented was forever lurking in the deepest recesses of his energetic body and mind.

Yesterday, she had taken a fancy to journey to a portion of land far to the north and many miles from their hamlet, a place never before explored by the pair. True, it was a beautiful day and any peril seemed slight, yet Diarmaid was hard pressed to dissuade her brusque, reckless spurt on the back of her beautiful Celabrar.

The steed had developed a tender hoof and the Irishman was concerned that Estrella could become stranded on some slender point of land with a lame horse. He had tried to explain his misgivings, yet the capricious woman, daring him with a defiant swing of her own mane of black hair, brashly rode off before him, laughing her passage up the beach, seemingly in a manner of spite. These were the qualities he could not fathom. Were all young women as impetuous and self-serving? He had no experience on which to base comparison.

Actually it had entirely worked out and once again to her satisfaction. When they reached a far cove, miles from the village, it was she who gently bathed and tended Celabrar's hoof in healing salt waters, all the while sporting her wicked smile and a will he thought he might never understand.

They had found another quiet, sandy bay, secluded and sheltered from the elements, with its small, wooded forest adjoining. The birds sang exquisitely here and the languorous day of love turned into one of the most beautiful in their turbulent courtship, further giving pattern to Estrella's will, he judged. How easily her every action became some plenteous bonus to her favor.

Hans and Count Pedro were still soundly asleep as he made his way out the deerskin flap of the hogan onto the peaceful, dewy ground. The village itself was just beginning to come alive with the soft stir of women preparing the morning meal and a child cooing and babbling somewhere in the expanse of neatly spaced hogans. A year of my life, Diarmaid mused, and here in such agreeable surroundings.

Never in all the months of living with the brown men had he detected any sense of rancor, jealousy or animosity. Their natures were absolutely serene as compared to the people of the other continent and he often thought long and mightily on the fact. How, when they had so little of material pleasures, could they be so uncomplaining, so gratified with their lot? Was it that having never seen the other way, and not having to deal with sordid commerce and avarice that this simple life was the best of all world's for any man? Yet Estrella longed so for her former ways. Could they possibly be as grand as she remembered or was the unattainable always the desired craving? He had much to sort out his reasoning before he gave himself up entirely to this woman.

Vaguely from some far off memory, those words taught to him by brother Clare, unmistakably now so long ago, winged lilting through his head. Good Clare had insisted he commit judgments of the great saints to memory, and presently one maxim in particular coursed in his brain as he stood gazing out over the waking village, today bathed in a fine petal-pink light of early daybreak.

"Law is twofold—natural and written. The natural law is in the heart, the written law on tables. All men are under the natural law." St. Ambrose, Bishop of Milan, (340-397)

Here, his God had permitted these beautiful children, in His infinite providence, to recognize only the natural law. They had no understanding of selfishness, lust, hate or bitterness. Those concepts were learned and unknown to these natives and to remain so until other men, who formed such opinions, made themselves a part of this paradise. Diarmaid fervently hoped that day might never come, despite all of Estrella's yearnings.

Part III

Magh Mell

MAGH MELL—the invisible world, land of the unseen—was usually separated from all human life by water. This could be a lake or an ocean, but a body which by some means must be crossed. In Pagan days the Celt in Ireland visualized several fairy lands: Tir-na n Og, the Country of Youth; Tir Tairngiri, the Country of Promise; Magh Argatonel, the Silver Cloud Plain; Magh Mell, the Plain of Honey.

Magh Mell was envisioned and existed on an island or group of islands ... or was seen by some as a fair, flowery plain, visible only to eyes which are opened under the waves of the sea.

❖ *Deliverance*

Huge, opaque cloud formations encircled the handsome Spanish galleon, Santa Rosa, as it rode unrestricted in the choppy seas just outside a warm gulf stream, so clearly recognized for its deep blue band of waters, yet these puffy, rain-filled vapors made the business of chancing a landfall on this particular morning in late March quite impossible.

Captain Torres was tense, although he in no way conveyed this image to his crew. This perilous coast of the new world had already cost him dearly. His beloved brother had been lost to it just one year ago as he commanded a similar Spanish vessel named The Annunciation. Word of that disaster had been reported by two adrift seaman, rescued from the wild sea after their prayers for survival were answered by a passing French ship, and the full account made known to him only three months ago when the malnourished sailors finally found their way to their homes in Spain. Now he had been selected to see if any others had survived, and this was his hazardous mission off the shore of this nameless land, for The Annunciation's consignment was one which his king, Philip IV, prized highly.

As for his own brother Luis, there was no hope of his being alive, for the rescued seaman swore they saw him perish beneath the ship and with their own eyes bore testimony to the fact. They did know, however, that the king's treasured cargo, namely, two women of the court and a nobleman, were set into the wild sea in a skiff only moments before The Annunciation capsized in that furious gale, and thus they had no certain knowledge of their fate. They also knew the ship was in the vicinity of these dreaded shoals when the disaster occurred; this coast that the sailors secretly termed, "Butcher Banks".

How, he wondered, had the vessel been blown so far off course. His brother was a most able captain and his destination was Baracoa, from where he had just embarked, far to the south, in Cuba. It must have been a terrible winter storm to bring them so far off course.

The governor there, Hernando de Altoras, had welcomed him warmly on his visit to that port only weeks before, regaling him with rare foodstuffs and gifts, begging him to search diligently for the governor's intended bride and her companions.

Captain Miguel Torres suppressed a chuckle as he smiled at the thought of a "bride" for the elderly, paunchy, grey-headed widower-governor with the bulging eyes, who seemed better suited for great-grandchildren or even the crypt than to be wedded to a beautiful young noblewoman. Perhaps the maiden was spared a fate worse than a watery death!

From his vantage point on the uppermost deck, he peered up at the shifting clouds to see that a change in the weather was fast approaching. This new world and all its frenzied sea was one he did not favor; his own normal trade route, bounding the calmer coast of Spain and France was much more to his liking. He would rather brave the threat of its warships than this ghostly coast. Yet he must explore its shoreline painstakingly and when finally satisfied that the king's favorite was not to be found, he could return to more quiet realm, in console of his brokenhearted mother on the loss of her only other son.

He stared long in the direction of landfall, yet still could see nothing of the undistinguished low, lying shore. He had been to this same strand only once in earlier years as a young ensign and even then had dreaded its murderous shoals and treacherous surge, for many a Spanish galleon had been lost to its watery graveyard.

But now, at last, the clouds were parting and a fresh breeze blew from the east, rapidly calming the sea. Yes, it was decisively time to get on with the decreed exploration and only then might he, Captain Miguel Torres, be headed homeward and back to Spain.

Island Thoughts

Count Pedro had slept late this morning. He awoke to find himself alone in the hogan, the sun already warm on the skins above his head. It was a fruitless life to be sure, for unless one was inventive, or made his own employment one with the pursuits of the natives, it remained a lazy existence. How luxurious it had always seemed at court, to lie in bed late into the day amid the silkiest of sheets and to be waited upon by the diverse servants serving only your pleasure. Here he might stay on his couch for as long as he wished, his essential needs were still taken care of, and yet without the alluring excitement in the conspiracies and intrigues of the court, idle repose now had somehow lost its sumptuous sensation.

He too, was well aware that today was the anniversary of his arrival on this shore, and it gave him stimulus to think about all future life. Would it be desirable that he too should take a local maiden for a bride and settle into a family style existence? It had certainly worked well for the Dutchman, Jochim, or so it seemed. He observed the plump man daily with his merry bride, apparently content and secure, for it was evident to all that soon they would become parents of a child and this fact only added to the former seafarer's pride and exuberance. With only one life to live, would the prospect be so boring or onerous, or far beneath the dignity he felt must be maintained ... he wondered?

Yet today was one which he would devote to the project envisioned by him for some nights. He must pursue the mission of exploration for any vessels ploughing this coast for one last course before he made any decision to settle down among the heathens, for he did not quite share the felicity of a Diarmaid. He had been taught that class distinctions held precise position in the scenario of his life and thus it was becoming increasingly more difficult for him to accustom himself into this world of such boring simplicity and union.

He dressed carefully and leisurely, for he must still be counted as a royal emissary, should he, by some miracle come across a search party. He had industriously repaired his original finery in which he was cast unto this shore, and today put on each piece of velvet and lace with particular sensory pleasure. Standing at last, tall, lean and arrayed, he swept his elongated, bony fingers through the thinning hair in a swell of imperious opulence and straightening his feathered tam upon the slick, dark head, proceeded forth in a style befitting this rakish courier to a reigning king.

******

Maria lay motionless on her bed in the stillness of the lodge. Estrella had slipped out much earlier, as was her habit ever since the steeds arrived on the island. Maria's bones particularly ached today. She was notably conscious of her legs feeling heavy and ancient as she guessed it was once again the change of the seasons which made her anguish so. After all, now in her forties, she was almost elderly, she reasoned, if only to herself, and she wondered if these brown persons were as old, for there was no way of perceiving age here except in lined faces and bent bodies.

Maria's entire life had been one of service to royalty and it was only in the last years that regret of a kind had set in. By some trick of fate she could have been born an Estrella or of equivalent noble birth. Her appearance had been what some might have considered beautiful in her day with her large, dark eyes and shining hair. Had she not been sold into the service of the court by her parents at the tender age of fourteen, she might have been anything she wished to be! Yet how foolish it was now to let her mind wander to such fantasies; the remainder of her life was destined to be only what it had become, a daily ritual of keeping Estrella's personal belongings, few as they were, in immaculate order and to see to her lady's physical needs. There was nothing else to occupy her time and now with the girl out of their lodging for most of every day with Diarmaid, her own lot was lamentable indeed. There had been, at the very first, after coming here, the energy of new environs with these bizarre peoples of interest to her, yet soon life had taken on a lackluster character, and she could discover no way to break the stupor of her existence.

Finally, with laborious effort, she placed her naked feet upon the brown, mat strewn floor and pulled her painful body upright. She too, was aware that a year had intervened since that terrible clash with the sea, and she calculated life was to be merely one year upon another of this same employment until the day she died.

******

Hans was off to the hogan nearby, were food was being prepared, soon after he arose this morning. He was a corpulent man and the prospect of nourishment in the early morn was always pleasurable promise. The victuals, readied with each sunrise were simple fare to be sure, yet still more appealing than this rough seaman had been accustomed to in the twenty and more years aboard vessels of the Dutch fleet.

He was particularly fond of the maize around which each meal was molded, and the attention and geniality of one brown lass had singularly caught his eye, as well as his solid reasoning. Perhaps as Diarmaid said, they were destined to remain here forever, never again to be found; was it a sin in that case to take a wife as his cousin Jochim had done, despite his family at home? By now they were surely convinced of his death in the sea and perhaps his own Matilda had herself taken a new husband for the sake of the children and her own loneliness. He could not blame her if she had! He moved his great body forward expectantly to be served his sunrise meal by the agreeable and timorous maiden, Temsina.

New Sails

March winds buffeted the count, moving him wildly to and fro across the beach, stinging microscopic grains of sand into his squinted eyes, so much so, that it became nearly impossible for him to scan the water's edge, much less a broad expanse of ocean. He wondered if his noble quest, seeming so reasonable when in the placid village this morning, had not after all been frivolity as he plodded on. He drew his cape tightly about the lean body for concern he could be blown abroad, himself.

He had walked the same length of open beach, as nearly as he could remember, to where they, the six had landed one year ago. There was no longer any ruin or remnant of their months of habitation, yet by the clear signs of forest and cove, he determined the place quite accurately. It was a long walk to this side of the island's windy beach and although the temperature was not frigid, the biting winds could soon force him to abandon his probe. How futile now it all seemed to him, after all. Nothing should be worth this chaffing, cutting torment of gale.

It was exactly at the moment that he decided to turn his form around and make his way back to more tranquil quarters that his aching eyes caught just a glimpse of thin fragment of white on the line of horizon. He stopped dead in his course to place a hand to his brow, now soaked with sea salt. Could it be only the flutter of gulls that he had mistaken so many times before in his eagerness to discern a vessel on the swells? No! It was moving closer and it could be none other than the sails of a ship, despite his agonized, drooping eyelids. Desperately, he wondered how he might make contact. It seemed so peculiar, that on the very day he chose to begin his search after so many months of regret, he should sight the very revelation of his illusion. It had to be destiny! This was a signal to all of them ... home... and to him, essentially, eventually, Spain!

******

The count's first impulse of building a bonfire for their notice had been quickly discarded as he remembered the force of the gusts. No fire would stay lit in such a gale. But what else could gain their attention? Immediately running to the pine woodlands which bordered the beach, he chose the piece of dune which stood highest among them, and frantically climbing the tallest, windswept tree, he spread his purple cloak out upon its branches in the hope it would catch the eye of some sailor aboard and appear evidence to be investigated. It took all the stamina he could muster to remain among its barbed branches while the galleon came ever nearer, finally sailing precisely parallel to the portion of beach to which he clung. Then ultimately, to his elation, he saw a boat lowered and a party of seamen work their way through the grinding surf, making straight for him.

By God, they were Spanish and what joyful reunion ensued when they ultimately beached their craft as he ran at full speed to greet them. The hasty speech that followed was happy and excited. The seamen seemed as jubilant upon finding the prize they sought, which each man had deemed as foolhardy, as was this regal emissary. How gratified he felt to have garbed himself in his royal finery, for the homage paid him now was dividend indeed for his trouble. Clearly the sailors lost no time placing him into the skiff and making steady for the sailing ship, so that he might meet with their captain straightaway.

Oh, how wonderful it was to once again see another male Spanish face and become acquainted to one's own countryman. Miguel Torres was delighted that Count Pedro de Mendenez was discovered, to be sure, for it not only meant a great prize for himself upon his return, but it assured him of being able to weigh anchor extremely soon to begin the long journey home, by way of Baracoa.

The seas had settled tolerably as the Spaniards spoke of all that had gone on during the year following the great storm which sank Miguel's brother, the count's pragmatic captain, aboard

Annunciation. It was an hour filled with food, wine and diverse pleasure for Count Pedro, yet as the sun began to lower in the western sky, he ultimately realized that he must fulfill his obligation to his Spanish companions remaining at the village. Then he too, would be lauded and compensated for his bravery and gallantry in finally depositing Estrella into the hands of the impassioned governor in Cuba. The count's beady eyes were bright in thoughts of the glory of it all. He was a genuine luminary, a hero, by God's grace, and there was no telling what the king might now do for him. Visions of gold and wealth untold, appeared before him and it was with real regret that he once more accompanied the band of seamen into the skiff to return to the shore and on to the village. He would now alert Estrella and Maria and whoever other of the survivors that might wish to accompany them in return to a life of distinct luxury and pleasure!

Magh Mell

The object of all this scenario was, at this very moment in the arms of her lover, Diarmaid. For an entire day, the two had secreted themselves amongst tall, cool pines in the lush cove, found so recently and far to the north of the village, and this time with each other's full submission.

"I like not to think of what this life would be if we had not been shipwrecked in that storm and made hostage of this same isle, one year ago, sweet Diarmaid."

Estrella seemed such a different creature, thought the contented, lounging Irishman, when she was altogether alone with him and away from all other memory of former days in Spain. Presently, he lay with his blonde head snuggled deeply into the folds of her lap, gazing skyward at a lone heron lazily soaring above the tallest of this small, exceptional and perfect forest and glade.

"I so not wish to consider it either, Estrella. We are indeed now in *Magh Mell*, that fairyland of wonder of which most men only dream. We have the best of all world's with simply our love to give and to receive from the other. What other blessing could any mortal desire?"

They had come here by the first light and had passionately given each other their devotion over and over again with each passing hour. Now it was almost twilight and the enchantment grew no less, only perhaps heightened by the very ardor of its eagerness. She was soft and pliant when alone with him, as though her willfulness was but the thorny ploy for others to view. Finally after the day of heated energy, Estrella sat tranquil and untroubled as she suddenly astonished him with her speech.

"I feel today marks a notable point in our time on earth. With one year gone, I too, am beginning to realize that, as you have said from the very first, there is small chance we shall be found and taken elsewhere. Therefore, my darling, I am telling you today that I will do as you wish, I desire to have Chief Croanatoa confirm and sanction our devotion with a ceremony so that we may live together in our own hogan unashamed before the entire company. What I am telling you, is, I do love you, Diarmaid, and wish to become your bride."

It was perfection; the gentle warming breeze finding these two twined, much as a strong vine encircles the trunk of the young birch, nearly choking the life from it, yet gaining total subsistence pulled from its vigorous solid form. Diarmaid and Estrella were finally altogether, one.

❦ *Lost and Found*

The news with which they returned so happily, turned to be but contentious tenor to the uproarious, festive mood attending their comrades in the village. Maria sat, with beaming face, her form crazily crooked atop an upturned cask, so unlike her habitual staid appearance that Estrella immediately knew something was amiss, even before she spied Count Pedro amid the crude seamen as they were being explored, petted and celebrated by the natives.

For there, in the center of the hamlet, six fearless Spanish seamen stood around the thin count, most notable by their fleshy abundance.

A miracle, perceived Estrella, they were discovered and on the very day of the anniversary, a dazzling omen to be sure; all thoughts of a life inhabiting this island quickly flew from her raven head as she moved agilely and boldly into the coarse assemblage.

******

Following the complete realization, there was little time to choose sides. Hans, Maria and the count were already gathering their few pitiful possessions from the lodges, even as the sailors encouraged them to make haste in reaching the shore by nightfall in order they all return to the galleon.

Diarmaid, through all the ferocity of the enterprise, stood as a dumb observer, shocked and speechless. In the space of one afternoon he had gained his bride and now it seemed as though he was to lose her. With a solicitous tug to her sleeve, he gained Estrella's attention and they moved into her hogan for quiet words.

"You would leave me now... you would go to Barocoa to become the bride of the governor?"

His face was colorless and wretched. Estrella had not seen the stalwart, ruddy Irishman as dispirited in all the months she had known him. She felt a complex sympathy and a unique compassion for this young man she had come to esteem, and yet how could she abandon the whole purpose of her expedition with true release so close at hand.

"I am torn in two, dear Diarmaid. You must come with us and leave this land, then we shall find some manner of our coming together in a world away from here; surely there will be some way in which we can still be united.

I do not wish to give you up, now that we have found each other, yet it is my duty to fulfill the destiny waiting for me. Can you understand ... it is our one chance ... for the remainder of our lives, to leave this place. Surely you would not expect me to stay now when deliverance is at hand?"

Estrella's eyes flashed with ferocity. She seemed caught up in the energy of her companions who were rushing wildly about in preparation for their journey.

"I have long ago made my decision, Estrella, I wish to become portion of this land and live out my days here. Possessing only a part of you would in no way be acceptable. I take it, that is what you are suggesting?"

Diarmaid did not look into her face, but out into the broad meadow that bordered her dwelling. The final rays of sun were setting upon a peaceful field with its silent birds hovering over the ground in the expectancy of night. Bran stood alert and attentive aside his disturbed master, sensing some crisis was at hand.

Piercing the composure of the moment, came the loud, incautious voice of Count Pedro for Estrella.

"Where are you, Estrella, we must be on our way, forthwith. The crew is ready to lead us to the galleon. Hurry now, this is our one chance!"

Estrella suddenly flung herself into Diarmaids arms. "I cannot leave you so, oh, Diarmaid, my true love, come with us, at least to the shore to see us aboard. We must also rope *Celabrar,* for I will take him with me. He has become portion of my life, likewise."

This woman was as bizarre in her reasoning now as Diarmaid had viewed her in the months past.

"If you do not wish to spend your remaining days with me, Estrella, then depart from my sight this moment. I cannot bear your vacillating nature for one more occurrence."

He turned then and left the hogan, striding swiftly into his own, Bran at his heels, leaving her standing alone, irate and shaken. There must be some avenue where she could have her will obeyed by this man, yet still keep her own way.

Estrella stamped her foot on the dusty earth and ground in her heel.

Flight

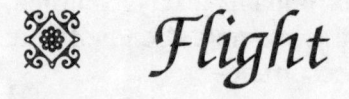

The rain was coming down steadily now. It moved in eerie, sheet-like passes above his head along with the powerful wind squalls accompanying it. Diarmaid could take his only pleasure in the fact that he was safe and dry in the snug hogan and that marginally. By now, in the middle of this dark night, Estrella and her group of sojourners should be safely aboard the Spanish galleon and weighing anchor for Cuba. His own life had taken on uncommon and cheerless continuance. He could not envision when it might again be joyful.

A crack of thunder and a sky alight with bolts of lightning made it abundantly clear there would be little sleep this night. He suddenly realized there were not even companions within this dwelling with whom he could converse on matters so slight. Bran by his side would be the brunt of any carping he might wish to sustain and yet to annoy the voiceless animal seemed cruel and inhuman treatment. No, he must live within this decision he had made with no regrets. The fact of being so close to love and union between two souls must be put forever from his young mind; that certainty of his own fate being ever without a female counterpart was again a real portion of his identity.

The night was as black as a raven's feather with neither the shipwrecked foursome nor the six bewildered seamen able to find a route through its murk, and when the storm broke loose shortly after midnight, it heightened their failure to make for the shore, complete.

Wet, frightened by the fury of the tempest and beleaguered by the thick forest, the band of ten could do nothing but plod on through its dense overgrowth hoping that their intuitive sense was leading them on toward the ocean.

The two women were riding Celebrar and with every crash of thunder the aroused steed reared his head and at times his front legs in gesture of stopping this futile journey through the tangled woodlands. Although Estrella would not concede her misgiving, Maria was beside herself with petition in loud pleading to return to the camp, at least until the daylight, however useless that entreaty might be, for not one of the saturated travelers knew their whereabouts.

It was a crestfallen band then, who found themselves at sun's rays only a meadow away from the village they had left at yesterday's nightfall. Somehow, they had journeyed in a gigantic circle, only to be once again where they had begun. All were wet and demoralized at this defeat, and unwilling to start out again without drying their clothing and taking some nourishment; that is except Estrella who felt revitalized with the coming of dawn. She assuredly knew her way to the beach with the brilliance of morn and on Celebrar could sprint to the ocean's shore in a matter of a half-hour. By now the seamen were sure another search party was out in their own pursuit and would be on the beach at daylight. It was they who urged Estrella to go on to tell their shipmates that by afternoon the entire party would be at the seashore, ready to board the Santa Rosa.

So it was with surprise that Diarmaid made his way into the provisions hogan, having finally wakened after a tortured sleep, following the dreadful storm, to find his old comrades and the six somber sailors cheerlessly sitting on the woven mats eating maize and fruit as the composed natives of his village again served them.

Estrella was nowhere to be seen and his first thought was that she alone was sailing on the ocean's tide, off to her betrothed, while these souls were somehow left behind to be forever his fellows, and she, absolutely lost to him. It was the same signal, to be sure, he was never to be the lover of the female, but only be compelled to possess a band of surly creatures as his duty, isolated on this island for his remainder of days; a destiny altogether inequitable and unjust in the sight of God.

Young Fool

Gaining the far side of the island with more speed than ever previously met, Estrella was an attractive sight, thought Miguel, captain of the Santa Rosa, the slim figure and flowing gown, astride the beautiful steed, made a handsome sight as her black hair whipped about an exquisite face, for she rode fearless and brisk up the beach at tide's edge to meet his second crew and himself.

Miguel had come personally this morning, as early as the sunrise, to find out why his first search party and passengers failed to board the waiting ship during the past night. His was a precarious position. Now that he had found the prize, he must hasten to get it aboard before the winds might change and hold him bonded there to have his ship dashed upon these unstable banks. His full thought was to get the little assembly aboard and be off. Now with the appearance of this beautiful woman astride her steed, he was to have his explanation.

Reaching the seven men standing about their skiff, pulled high upon the sandy beach, Estrella was quick to discern who was leader of the group for the rich braid he wore as mark of a Spanish sea captain. Taking him aside and out of earshot of the common seamen, Estrella rapidly revealed the reason for the delay. She was flushed from the gallop and the color in her cheeks made the commander feel a heated flush of coloration himself. It had been some months since he had viewed a specter as lovely, and he was initially and momentarily flustered as he attempted speech.

"Welcome, dear lady, we are gratified to find you and your party so well and robust. Your guardian, the count, has told me all of your woeful ordeal and now we are at your service to speed you and your party to our vessel, hastening to Baracoa and shelter. I have departed from your intended husband but a few weeks ago. He will be overjoyed at your salvation."

"This is the one reason I wished to come alone and to hear from your own mouth of the governor. You have met him then ... you have knowledge of his culture and of his person, ... that is, of his character and demeanor? What I am asking, Captain Miguel, is, what the man is truly like, what of his appearance and his fitness. Is he the treasure, the prize that all at the court have led me to believe? I have suffered greatly in the effort to attain this man."

Estrella was quick with her words, her intention most clear. The captain was amazed at her brazen behavior.

"You have observed his manner and countenance. No one in Spain could tell me this, and now there is the greatest, most decisive reason... I must know!"

Miguel was caught in a new dilemma of great proportion. Should he describe the man as virile, robust and appealing, it would only be a matter of weeks at sea and his analysis would be proved fallacious, for the paunchy, elderly, ruin of a mortal, who he knew the governor to be, would be seen in the flesh and what of Estrella's wrath when that truth were known. She could, with her standing in the realm, have him stripped of his rank and property. Yet, on the other hand, should he tell the truth, she might not wish to accompany him, and then his mission would be failed. Here too, he would feel the ire of king and court. His was a dismal and cautious choice to be sure.

"Let us sit over here in the shade of the trees for a moment, dear lady, a bit farther from my unsightly crew, and I will tell you what I know of Senor Hernando de Altoras."

Estrella was impatient, yet she did as Miguel wished, guiding Celebrar beneath the gnarled oaks, tying him to a branch so he might snooze in its shade.

"What is his appearance and how old of a man is he?"

These were the very two question that the captain feared that she would ask and yet it was a natural inquiry.

"He was most gracious and cordial to me in Baracoa and he is a ... a..well, let us say a most ... mature gentleman. As to his age, I am in perplexity to speculate. I should say he must be...well, say ... over fifty? ... if I am any judge."

Estrella could see by the way in which this most likely, straightforward sea captain was unable to look into her eyes as he spoke, that he was unquestionably not being candid, thus she added ten years to the figure he had given, then gasped and shivered as she calculated the pitiable prospect. At twenty-six, she could not see herself chained to such an elderly magistrate, no matter how generous and affable he might be. Oh, how had she been so deceived by the persons at court. They must surely have known this and kept the fact from her, or could it be that her own greed had closed her own ears to their dialogue? To be lady, perhaps nursemaid, to an aging, croaking old man was not what had brought her over the savage ocean, no matter who erred.

She turned on her heel in hot rage and buried her face in Celebrar's auburn mane. How could she have been taken for such an incredible, gullible fool!

Back at the village the few natives who served rations had departed the provisions hogan in favor of other appointed duties. Diarmaid was always amazed at the mild manner with which they could view current, abnormal episodes of these odd Europeans without so much as the flick of an eye. His brown friends had the uncommon capacity to be only their own person, to not allow worldly concerns any place where they applied to reality separate from their lives. Oh if only all mankind could learn from these so called "savages" reasoned the Irishman.

The six seamen were readying themselves outside the hogan, eager to be on their way to the beach, as were Count Pedro, Hans and Maria. When Diarmaid determined that the only manner in which the senior, Maria was to reach the ship, accompanied by the men, was to plod her own way through the heavy underbrush, he gallantly offered his own steed, Loch Derg, for her to ride upon, and himself as guide so that the party would not be lost afresh in the perplexing forest.

He had come to value Maria as a charitable, speechless friend because of her patience with her mistress and himself. A trek of such length would be exhausting for the woman.

The little band found no displeasure in Diarmaid's proposal, and they were off within moments of his placing Maria on his trusted mount. With the bright Bran bounding by their sides, the ten nomads set off into the budding morn.

❖ *The Choice*

Estrella said no more to Miguel de Torres, for she needed time to think. It could only be a matter of a few hours and the party would be here ready to row for the vessel and on to Cuba; precious little time to decide what course she must initiate for herself. As she viewed the coarse seamen, waiting about the skiff, grizzled and tough, she thought of the firm, clear, young skin of her Diarmaid, of his distinct unspoiled laughter and his thick, tawny crown of tousled hair. She envisioned his blue, lucent eyes that flashed when he was excited and his muscular, powerful arms having the power to lift her own body high above his head when he wished to do so.

How could she chance an unknown, archaic creature for a known, unspoiled man pulsing with life and who had already vowed his undying love for her. The balance seemed unequal to be sure. To take the ancient unknown for the virile, independent, desirable man was absurd, as she could plainly reflect. She sat on the gritty sand, sifting it idly through her fingers.

But how to get the count to permit her to stay and let the remainder of them depart? He had boasted only last evening of how he was finally to be loyally rewarded, as was befitting his post, for seeing his consignment to its destination, despite the delay. His manner had been forceful; how could Estrella manage to dissuade him. Impulsively she turned her back to the beach and to the distant crew while stretching her legs out before her to take the black and amber cask once more from its hiding place in the folds of her gown.

Opening it, she counted the treasure still remaining within, yes, here was a sizable fortune in gold and jewels. Secreted there too, safe in the lid, were the documents which indicated she, Estrella de Valazquez, was of noble birth; these were the papers which she must show to Governor de Altores upon her arrival to his shore, in proof that she was his intended bride, signed by King Philip himself; once lost, these could never again be retrieved. Without them, she was merely a Spanish woman, as ordinary as any other seen on the streets of Madrid or Toledo, yet on the other hand, free... free to be the person she presently desired to be ... free to become as one with Diarmaid and to finally abandon the lunatic mission on which she was sent.

An ingenious and calculating plan began forming in her mind, and now she had incredibly little time to accomplish it.

******

Meanwhile the winds began to pick up, the very forecast which Miguel Torres had dreaded. He sat on the prow of the beached skiff gazing skyward and then alternately out to his magnificent galleon riding the waves just within sight. He had given orders to his first mate that should a storm ensue while he and the remaining hands were on land, that he was to take the ship out to sea to ride out any squall, lest they take the chance of being dashed upon the shoals. Now his own concern was of being marooned on this forsaken strand of earth, and all for the rescue of these persons who seemed very unsure of their salvation anyway, or so it had seemed with this young woman, Estrella, especially when he had ultimately told her the age of her betrothed. His honesty, nearly betraying his conscience in telling her the entire truth, would have done no good, but only possibly delay the departure of the entire assembly for yet another period. No, better that he just skirted the truth and let the misgiving become complete on the other end where he was nearer to his final destination of Spain.

The wistful girl became very quiet after he made his half-truth known. She asked to be alone and he respected those wishes, yet as he silently watched her sitting despondently on the sand only twenty yards down the beach, he wondered what desperate thoughts filled her gorgeous head.

The rain began to fall once more as the party of ten were almost midway between the hamlet and the shore. An alert

Diarmaid knew by certain signs of the forest when they were precisely half-way. It started in mere droplets, falling softly through the sheltering trees, but in only moments the patter changed to driving sheets of water, cold and sharp. Diarmaid took off his own cloak to wrap about the huddled form of Maria, holding tightly to the bare back of Logh Derg, but the thin material was little protection from nature's onslaught.

He likened the sudden and fearful storms here on this island to the sporadic, wild, tempests which raged about the monastery when he was a child in Ireland. Then the blasts and downpours seemed they would never end. He remembered how he had feared their savage thunder, their frenzied lightning, and how it was Brother Joseph who would take the tiny child on his huge knee, sheltering him within the crook of his arm, tight into a rough sackcloth habit of grey fabric which all the monks wore, to tell him fanciful tales of exquisite provinces like Magh Mell, the plain of honey, or Tir-na n Og, the country of youth, until the tempest subsided and he was again calm and peaceful.

No real father could have been as understanding or loving, yet he was privileged to know many men who cared for him and calmed his childish fears. What role they all played in the making of the man was eternally bordering his thought. He constantly strove to do those things which he felt they might do in like situation, however difficult that now seemed, these many miles from their practical tutelage.

"I like not the looks of this storm, Diarmaid. Do you believe it will cause us again to be delayed in gaining the ship this day?"

It was Count Pedro who had sprinted ahead from his place at the rear of the company to raise his voice over the howl of wind and to speak into Diarmaid's moist ear.

"All we can do now, count, is advance onward. Perhaps the downpour will have done with itself by the time we reach the others. You know by now, how quickly this isle can change its breezy character."

Diarmaid felt no necessity for irrelevant conversation and so he moved rapidly and certainly ahead, and by so doing showed the count, his determination to energize them on to the beach.

❋ *Secrets Shared*

Maria of all the party was perhaps the most thankful to finally gain the ocean's shore. It was with real relief that she permitted the seamen to assist her in dismounting Loch Derg and to fall wearily into Estrella's waiting arms. The attachment between the women had become curiously bountiful during these twelve long months. It was no longer the mistress and the groveling, obedient servant seen as they departed the Spanish shore, but now they shared nearly a familial bond, one which finally held the two women in a unique mellowness of comradeship.

The rain had decisively ceased as they gained the ocean, only a fine mist was falling, almost undetected amidst the salt spray of the seashore. Now the two groups merged and it was a sizable company that stared out into the horizon for the ship which had brought most of them to this barren strip. True to his captain's orders, the mate had taken the galleon far out into the depths, and it was Captain Miguel himself who offered that it could be the next morning before they might catch sight of it once more, for the storm seemed to travel eastward and the Santa Rosa was held off the coast for yet another night.

With that assertion, the seamen readied their skiffs to make assorted shelter for another long night to come. By tipping and turning them against the prevailing wind, they made lean-to's of sorts and spread their outer clothing upon the sand as a floor. Giving over one boat to the found survivors and their captain, they huddled, grumbling under the remaining one themselves. Thus the assemblage of some eighteen souls camped out upon the open beach for one more, seemingly, endless night.

Straightaway, Diarmaid determined that he would see this piteous circumstance to its conclusion and settled himself at the far end of the shelter with Bran by his side. The entire party had only a small pailful of rations to be shared among them, leaving all the stomachs thereabouts rumbling with discontent.

Maria and Estrella huddled themselves in the center of the boat sanctuary, completely occupied in dialogue in their native tongue with intense rapidity. They seemed oblivious to the others, and it was clear that Maria was dissenting some certitude which Estrella put forth. They spoke in hushed tones so no one could overhear.

"It is the only way ... the only course I have, Maria. You must accept this plan I've set for you and I. Think now, clearly it is the only method by which either of us can find happiness ... Listen, Captain Torres tells me that the governor has sent refined women's clothing and gowns aboard the ship on the possibility that we should be found. It will be a matter of weeks before you are landed in Cuba and by that time you will be able to pamper yourself to become most presentable for the nobleman. Think of it, dear heart, it will be a life of ease and pleasure for you in all your remaining days. None can find out about the interchange, for you shall pay the count these many golden ducats to hold his tongue, once you are aboard. They can do me no good here and too, he will fear for his own petty life should he betray us. The answer for your appearance of being a bit older than what the governor expects is easily resolved by saying that a year on a barren island has been most hard on you. But conclude, Maria, you are a delicate, beautiful woman still, and he will see that in your manner and bearing. Moreover, you will possess these documents which proclaim you to be Estrella de Valazquez for all the world to scrutinize. No one can doubt their authenticity. So you see, Maria, you shall become me and I shall remain here, only a humble Spanish woman enabled to live with my lover till my dying day on this Magh Mell. It is a pragmatic plan, do you see? As to an explanation of your whereabouts, you shall say Maria was lost to the sea in the storm which sunk the Annunciation. We must, however, not make our plan known until the count and you are safely under sail. I will manage to find passage in the other skiff and he will not know I am missing until it is all too late. If we tell Count Pedro ahead of time, he will insist that I go to Cuba, but this way, once at sea there will be nothing he can do! You shall do it for me Maria, you shall."

Estrella's eyes were as coals burning with fire when she spoke. Maria could not remember another time when she had been as unyielding and aglow, and there certainly had been many to compare, no, she knew it was no use to dissuade her mistress in this, the last of their adventurous lives together.

Hoax

It was the count who finally interrupted their conversation. He bade Estrella walk with him a way up the beach that he might speak with her alone, and that idea fit exactly into Estrella's enormous plot. She would impress him with her eagerness to be away. Instantly, she stood up and acquiesced to his invitation. The rain and winds had nearly subsided and with the final rays of light they strode on the shore as sea maws swooped and screeched about their dark heads.

"Well now my dear Estrella, we are finally favored by the gods with the fortune such as we have long coveted. By the morning we will be off with the wind and on to Cuba."

Estrella observed that the count had once more assumed his imperious airs and those adamant mannerisms which she had become so accustomed to in Spain. He curiously, in the past twenty four hours, had become the commanding courtesan she had known before their island episode. His bearing was full of authority and had she not been full of her own secret knowledge of her soon to be enacted scenario, she would have been belligerent at such arrogance, however now she was happy to feign complete allegiance to his every whim, so to keep him ignorant of any turn in her intention.

"It has been a long year for all of us, dear Pedro and for we two especially, I think. The others were not accustomed to the splendor in which we shared. It will be excellent, indeed, to be off this strand and on to civilized society."

Estrella walked closely by the tall count's side, uttering, echoing and nodding with his words as if in complete concurrence with his notions. He must not for one instant believe anything else than her complete desire and appetite for their flight from this island, and as soon as possible. This was essential for the accomplishment of her undertaking.

Thick, dark clouds moved boldly with the evening winds to display a ripe moon shining down brightly on the pair as they strode far from the others, deep in conversation. Estrella pulled her cape up close about neck and cheek to secret her face from the piercing eyes, pretending to block a freshened breeze, yet in reality in endeavor to hide her beaming, devilish visage from his intense view.

❈ *Final Deception*

It was a long, restless night for all assembled on that narrow strip of island, but for Estrella it was a sleep she did not covet. Her mind raced joyfully through each dark hour, for she could just glimpse the tawny head of her Diarmaid who slept at the far end of the skiff's shelter as the full moon's rays caught its fine, bright blonde gleam.

She had no wish to tell him of her plan. If he knew, she felt that perhaps the alchemy might be broken and the concept would not succeed. She must work all the intricacies alone, for it must go off without blunder. Everything ... her entire future life was to depend on these next hours, here on this slender beach.

Yet she saw no reason to be without him on this, the last night he believed they would ever be together? With delicate movement Estrella slipped from beneath the wooden shelter of the skiff, carefully moving Maria's slim hand that lay upon her shoulder, and in a near crawl exited its refuge to move noiselessly toward the far end of the craft where Diarmaid slept fitfully.

It must have been nearing two o'clock in the morning and all of the tired crew, captain and friends were in deep slumber, their snoring seeming to pause coincident with each wave of the sea's surge, so close at hand. Estrella had no difficulty reaching Diarmaid's side without waking the others.

"Diarmaid, darling," she whispered placing her small hand to his cheek. "It is Estrella ... shush now, for I do not want to wake anyone."

His sleep was light and the first touch of her palm had him awake and vital.

"I thought I was hearing my name in my dream. Precious Estrella, I am glad you have come to me."

His voice was a hoarse whisper and she covered his mouth with her slim fingers, lest he say more.

Taking his hand in her own, she pulled on it, indicating she wished him to get to his feet, then standing herself, she guided him away from the group and off toward the shelter of live oaks some twenty yards up the beach and under the protection of a dune.

There they fell to their knees and embraced in that desperate manner of parting and yet in the same movement, of melancholy reunion.

Neither spoke, but remained there in the all encompassing grasp of the other until their breaths were short and they could no longer hold the other upright as the balance of their bodies grew unstable with the ferocity of their ardor. For a long time, after finally sitting in unison on the hard, cold sand, no sound was heard, only the relentless roar of the waves slapping the beach below them. What hopeful thoughts rushed through Diarmaid's brain in those wordless moments was but speculative confusion, for a poignant longing rose and fell with the swells as Estrella took from him and at the same time gave in the same evidence of lavish devotion.

"I have not slept, this entire night, dear Dove, and the viewing of your gorgeous person only feet from me under the shelter was finally more than I could endure. Let us share these final hours together for what they will mean to us in the remainder of our lives."

So saying, Estrella reached up and pulled his confused head again into her warm lap as she had done so many times when they were alone together. He was as mystified and whirling from this headstrong woman as he had been countless times before, yet he did not contest her movement, only succumbed entirely to her wiles as in those hundred times earlier.

Again no words were voiced and it was plain to the two that a myriad of sounds of animals and birds of the forest behind them was becoming increasingly audible as the dawn approached.

Estrella could hear each of nature's voices so plainly and with such rapture that it made her pure resolve absolute with every sound, and yet there was an impudence within her which could not yet allow this man to sense her choice for all their destinies.

That taunting, teasing trait of a rebellious spirit made these but puzzling, stolen moments with her beloved, and only became the more appealing to her astounding ego. This now was the moment that she knew her spell was made complete.

Lastly, as they sat conscious of every movement, every vibration in the trees, unseen, at their backs, Estrella smoothed his golden, silky hair and bent forward to place a cool cheek against Diarmaid's own. Then she whispered the ancient poem which he had taught to her as a portion of his own heritage:

> "Sleep a little, a little little,
>   for thou needst not fear the least,
>   lad to whom I have given love,
>   son of O Duibhne, Diarmaid.
>
> I will watch over thee the while.
>   Tonight the grouse sleepth not
>   up in the stormy heaths of the height,
>   sweet is the sound of her clear cry:
>   between the streamlets she does not sleep.
>   ...Sleep a little.

******

True to Captain Torres's belief, with the first rays of the day the Santa Rosa was sighted, silhouetted by the rising sun from an eastern sky and the gritty crew set up a wild cheer, then commenced to right the skiffs in preparation to set to sea with their consignment of foreigners.

These were the moments which were crucial to Estrella's strategy. Now, once more back in her place beneath the skiff, she quickly arose, strode to the trees and unhitched Celebar to seek out the second mate who would tie him to the aft of her skiff so that the horse could swim behind it to the ship.

Estrella knew that this act would establish in everyone's mind, including the count's, that she had full intention of departing this island. She and Celebar were as one body in the way she cared for the creature; she knew it was inconceivable that anyone would believe she could part with her beautiful stallion. In fact, it finally confirmed to Diarmaid's brain that she was assuredly leaving their Magh Mell, even though he held out faint hope that she could change her mind in these last moments, because of the night just gone.

There was the bustle of placing the few possessions aboard the skiffs which stood some ten feet apart, then the boarding which Captain Torres directed. Maria and Count Pedro were placed in the center of six oarsmen in the forward craft which was already plowing the incoming surge, with its sailors so eager to be off.

Placing Hans and himself in the center of the second skiff, the Captain held out his hand to Estrella and seated her in the aft portion of his boat, so that she might be close to the animal following on its rope tether. Then, they too were pulled into the crashing waves and in only an instant were full abreast an azure sea; Celebrar scrambling and then finally swimming behind them.

It all happened so abruptly that Diarmaid was left standing alone on the beach and without any farewell kiss or embrace from Estrella who did not once look backward at the dispirited form standing there watching the boats move rapidly from his sight.

The skiff which held the count was making fleet time as was compared to the second with its added impediment of the beast struggling behind the stern. The first had nearly reached the Santa Rosa when Diarmaid decided to turn dejectedly to begin his trek home with Loch Derg and Bran, finding it unbearable to view this sight of her departure.

It was just as he took his last glimpse of Estrella's dark head, almost lost to view among the tossing waves, that he thought he saw something bizarre. Estrella was standing upright in the skiff with a shiny metal object in her hand, and as suddenly she bent over the stern, made a circular motion with her arm and as one body, threw herself into the dashing waves, her slim arms grasping tight about the neck of her beautiful stallion. He stood horrified as he saw the horse turn and attempt to swim for the shore, Estrella bobbing helplessly among the swells, sometimes seen and at other times lost beneath their energy.

He wanted to call to those in the skiff. Why didn't they turn and try to rescue his darling? His voice strangled in his throat with the horror of the scene. Yet, just as he thought all was lost and that Estrella had committed that lamentable act which would lose her to all of life forever, the majestic, powerful Celebrar emerged from the foaming surf with Diarmaid's beloved still clinging to his massive neck and flowing mane. She fell hard to the beach, the white foam lapping at her figure, her long hair all tangled and wild about the pale face.

Diarmaid rushed to her side as she rolled over in the froth and smiled up wickedly into his fearful face.

"Did you think that I would leave my gorgeous Diarmaid for any other pleasure this world might offer?"

To his incredulity, she just lay there on the sand, the warm waters dancing all about her body as he bent down to pull her raven, Spanish Gypsy head into his bare arms.

"By now I should know... I must realize that I can never, ever believe you, you glorious, wild being ... as for sleep ... my beautiful, irresponsible, dramatic Estrella, I know but one consummate thing, I shall never sleep...

alone again!

THE END